BROKEN CHILD

BROKEN WOMAN

Written by Charles Lee Robinson Jr. & Elaine Denise Robinson

Broken Child Broken Woman

Charles Lee Robinson Jr. & Elaine Denise Robinson

Copyright

Dedication

I would like to dedicate this book to all my family. My mom Elaine Denise Robinson wrote this book and I decided to continue her legacy by writing her story, and to all my supporters who believe in my work. I'd liked to dedicate to every young girl and young boy who has endured what's written in this book. I pray that you will overcome and live a normal life. I'd like to dedicate this book to my Grandmother, Shirley Johnson, she is a beautiful woman and I understand her hard times were a struggle, but she did her best with what she had. I would also like to dedicate this book to my Dad, Charlie Lee Robinson and my siblings, Celesteen Dawn Robinson, Patrice Perez, Deanna Robinson, and La Ron Deshawn Robinson.

ACKNOWLEDGEMENTS

First, I'd like to acknowledge God for giving me his perfect gift from above. To all my family, friends, and supporters, I thank you for your encouragement and motivation. I would like to acknowledge my Editor, Patricia Ann Dukes, and to all the authors who supported me: Dr. Allen Parker, Doreen S. Dunn-Berts, Themix Nixter. To my Aunts Willie Mae Sullins, Rose Mae Robinson, Everne Robinson, Brenda Robinson, Uncle Willie Robinson Jr., and my late Aunt and Uncle, Margarette Robinson and Henry Robinson. I want to acknowledge special friends, Oscar Beasley, Travis Biggham, James Love, Antoine Taylor, Quentin Postell Sr., Albert Sanchez, Sharita Calhoun, Monica Calhoun, Erica Calhoun, Day Day Calhoun, Man Man Calhoun, Shakira Terry, Theresa Tatum. I would like to thank my family and friends for being the core of my growth, and for being a very big part of my life. I wouldn't be the man I am today, if you all weren't a part of my life. To all of you I have not mentioned, you are not forgotten.

TABLE OF CONTENTS

FOOD FOR THOUGHT:

As I stare off into space, I wonder who is watching me...my life has been filled with hardship and despair...from day to day bad things happened to me, and I say it's not fair...my past haunts me...like a confused spirit embedded in my soul...it follows everywhere I go...I want to live in tranquility...but something won't let me have serenity nor peace...I am tempted everyday...so an anointed shield is what I seek...I know my life is being played out in two directions...so which way do I go...which choice do I make...that's why I have to make sure every move is great...As I stare off into space, I wonder who is watching me...will it change my faith or my destiny?

PROLOGUE

The beginning – We should start with the day of my birth. Not knowing anything, I was born with a clean slate, like everyone else I knew at that time. For many years, I heard and felt that someone was watching me, I often tried to tell people, but no one would listen. I said, "Mom, there's something I must tell you." However, that fell on a deaf ear or maybe she didn't want to believe it. I felt like an oddball; but where do I fit in when no one will listen to me? Something was always telling me someone was there watching me. My skin would crawl and I felt scared. I tried to shake this feeling of always being watched. I'd walk down the streets; I could feel the eyes everywhere I went. I'd say, "Who is that?" I asked, and I would never hear an answer. I started to see things happen and other things fall apart. I knew someone was there, but no one believed me. Things were beginning to make me scared, and someone told me God was watching me. I tried to make a move, and someone would take apart everything I worked hard on, and some would call it karma, but everyone else would say I was crazy. I would tell mom, "This is not a good day for you, so watch what you do," I said. My mother would come home and sure enough my intuition was right. She would say I had a bad day, and then she told the kids they were going to get in trouble, and they did. Like I said, I was an oddball and everyone would overlook it and no one knew what to do about it, but it was something I had to live with. Until this day, I questioned, "So what was I supposed to do with this ability?" I didn't know, all I knew was, when things were going to happen to others in my family; it did. This is where I came from, and can you change where you come from? People said I was weird, because I told them things were going to happen, and I was always feeling something; and it was right.

CHAPTER ONE – THE BEGINNING/I FEEL LIKE I'M BEING WATCHED

I was a sad broken little girl; nothing went right for me and I had no friends. Soon I would find friends, some good and some bad. Somehow, I felt there was going to be a death in our family and I tried to warn them something bad was about to happen, and I also knew when someone would get into trouble. My mother had to go to work every day. My brothers and sisters father was supposed to look after us. He would beat us and leave us alone for many hours, but he would always manage to be there when she got home. When I told her that he would beat us while she was at work, she became angry and she would tell me that it was my responsibility to keep my siblings safe, because mommy had to work. I felt broken; my life was never fun. I always felt hurt and pain. He'd get drunk and leave us alone. One day my brother was jumping from bed to bed and messing up the house; I knew something was going to happen. The beds were made of old iron, and he missed the whole bed and got stuck on a piece of iron. There was a large piece of iron sticking out of the bed on the side, when he missed the bed; my brother became impaled on that piece of metal. Blood was coming out of him fast. I called my auntie, who was upstairs, to tell her that my brother was dying and bleeding all over the bed. She called for help. The fire department and Paramedics arrived, they cut the part of the bed that was stuck in my brother, and put him on a stretcher and took him to the hospital. Shortly afterwards, my step dad came in the house all drunk, someone should have taken us, but I'm glad they didn't because we probably wouldn't have seen each other again. I don't know why they didn't take us; we would run up and down the streets like no one cared. This was the last straw when he wasn't there, when this happened to my brother. Mom worked hard and he didn't, and I absolutely had no clue as to why she would let him stay. All I knew, I was just a child that has been given adult responsibilities to help her out. It felt so unfair, mom was mad about what happened to my brother. She still had to work, and she cried that night. My brother was in the hospital for a while. My auntie kept us until she got sick, she became mentally ill, and I think she was slowly going crazy. When I was at her house, I saw when it started to happen, her words didn't make any sense, and she was seeing things that weren't there. She would run back and forth yelling, we looked at her and we were scared. I told mom, I will keep the kids safe, and something was wrong with auntie; because she talks to herself and yells and cry. My auntie had lost her mind and she was now living upstairs. She would just stare at us after that. I was feeling scared and I would scream, "What are you looking at?" She just looked at me with an evil smile. Sometimes I would just run pass her as she stood on the porch above. We didn't go up there anymore, we were left alone and our step dad would still leave. Auntie would say crazy things like, "Something is going to burn." I often heard her yelling crazy things and talking out of her head, jumping on the floor above or rocking in her old rocking chair. One night something told me there was going to be a fire in the house. I woke up and smelled something burning. I got everyone out, because there would have been a lot of lives lost due to this fire. I woke up all the people in the four apartments who were sleeping. I banged on their doors and they all ran outside. Twenty people were homeless from this fire, but alive. Who was that warning me; they had to have known the appending doom. Did that crazy lady start the fire which nearly killed all of us including herself? The events that happened after then would forever change my life. I felt like I was dealt a dirty hand, because so many things went wrong. I'm broken and I have a feeling something's going to happen. It scared me every time I told someone things were going to happen. When it came to past, it shook me to the core. There was a girl next door who had premonitions like me, her name was Liz. She said something in my home wasn't right, and my mom was going to get sick, and mom got sick. She told me someone will molest me in the future. I didn't know what that meant, but it came true. She was right about mom getting sick. Who was telling her these things about me and my family? I knew it and I felt it, she had psychic abilities like me, she foretold what would happen, how did she know this? My mom got sick and we had to go to a foster home. She knew this, and this was the worst time I ever had in my life; or so I thought. The woman who we were placed with was a doozey. She was a drunk, always yelling and cursing at her man. She would put us outside every day and tell us to go to the playground. It was summer break and they would give us free lunch. When she fed us, the food was nasty. She fed us cold hot dogs on buttered bread, never cooking us a good meal. There weren't any social workers during those days who would follow up and make home visits to make sure the foster children were safe and out of harm's way. Back then they would just give the foster parents the check that was supposed to be for taking care of us, but the check was used to support our foster mom's alcoholism. We had fun at the playground and we got dirty. Our foster mom was supposed to keep us, but we kept ourselves. We were dirty and our hair was not taken care of. It wasn't just me and my brothers and sisters, but the other foster kids too. She had ten children in her home, and that check was big. I kept my siblings with me. Sometimes we would go back to the house and try to get inside to eat any food we could find. Our mom would never treat us like this. She had me take care of my brothers and sisters while she worked, because her husband didn't stay with us like he told her he would. We lived better than this; we always had food and clean clothes to wear. I was told to do things older children should do. Sometimes the door was open, and she would be so drunk, I would take the kids inside and wash them. We ate what didn't have to be cooked. As soon as we would saw her waking up, we ran outside and then we acted like we wanted to come inside. She was so drunk; she didn't know that we were inside her house. Just before she told us it was bedtime; I would tell the kids to wash themselves. We had dirty clothes and were young and couldn't wash, but I did wash the few clothes we had. We would change, but she rarely washed our things. Some of the other kids just got into bed all sticky and nasty. She would wash clothes maybe once a week, for ten kids plus her own two. Many nights I cried, I wanted my mom back and the love she showed us. I would get mad with my step dad for being so mean to us. He would hit my mom and make her sad. I guess after you are beaten up so much, you lose track of who you are, but I always held myself together, I had to make sure we would all be in one piece when mom came back to get us. This was a nasty house with big rats running all around us. I kept asking why is this happening, where is all my family? Granny used to have many folks over, are they not my real family? I knew one day the rats would bite us, but didn't know which one or how many bites. They bit us at night, we didn't know if that old lady was aware of the rats, or she didn't care because she was getting paid. Every day we were told to get up and go to the playground, and she started her drinking and cussing. For hours, we would run, play, and get in the dirt. Some days we got in the little pool they had, and then they would feed us lunch. After lunch, we would go back to the house, we were sleeping and just needed someone to care for us; not her. No one came to see about us children. I lay awake at night wondering why. They told us my mom had a heart attack and we may never go home again. I prayed to God that someone in our family would come get us. All that family and no one would take us in, why? My granny would always have kin over, where were they? I was told my granny was sick, she couldn't take us, and maybe she got sick because my mom was sick. I'm feeling a certain way. We had a big family, aunties, and uncles, yet we are in foster care, why? Well, word got around to our cousin Zoe. She found out that we were getting mistreated in our foster home, and she came and rescued us. Rats were running everywhere and we were so scared at night. This house was never clean; there were rats in the kitchen, and everywhere in that house. They were so bold; they ran around the house in day light, but when the lights went out, they got worse. I could hear them scratching, running, and tearing at the trash can, soon I would fall asleep; wake up and it was another day. Why would anyone allow her to be a foster parent with this dirty house? We would be standing still, and sometimes a rat would run right by us. She was drunk and acted like she didn't see it. Until this day, I will not let a mouse/rat run around in my house, rats are bold; I've seen them attack. They will bite and keep biting; they are not scared of people. They were big sewer rats. One night all of us were in one big bed, and a big rat got into the bed with us. I knew because of the girls next to me began to scream. I pulled off the covers and the rat had bitten her, and her blood was in the bed. We all jumped out of the bed and so did the rat. Like I said, dirty little kids in a dirty bed, even the bitten girl was dirty, now bleeding all over and crying. The rat bit her sticky leg, she had eaten candy. The rat came into the bed many times while we slept. The rat must have been running around us. We all ran to this lady's room, only to find her so drunk, she couldn't do anything because we couldn't wake her up. The others and I ran outside screaming and yelling. The folks next door called the police. She was so drunk when the police came and finally woke her up. Our cousin was called and she took us to her house. I don't know what happened to that lady and the kids, but I was glad we were out of there. Zoe's house was a little better, because we did get food, but I had to beat my cousin's son off me every day. He didn't think blood/kin meant anything; he wanted sex and was always touching and kissing me. I would wake up with him all on me, and I would fight him off, I would cry and push him off me. Back then, I didn't know what sex was, but as I got older, I hated him for trying that with me, his blood cousin. I was so afraid of him. He would tell me I was so pretty and he wanted me. I just thought about what that meant, I had to run and keep myself away from incest. I started sleeping in my cousins' mom bedroom on a chair. I told her I needed to be near her, because I miss my mom and needed to be close to a mother figure. Mom got well and my prayers had been heard, and we were going home soon. Shortly afterwards, she came home. I knew I was truly being watched by my baby sisters' father. He moved in with us. He was supposed to be helping my mom out while she was getting well. He watched my every move, always feeling, and touching me in the wrong places like my cousin did. As time went by, mom got well and she was stronger. It was time to go back to school; our whole summer was a mess after she got sick.

Maybe we could get back on track, but he can't keep his eyes off me. It just doesn't feel right, why is he watching me? I couldn't tell mom. Would she believe me? Sometimes, I couldn't trust people like him. I knew something was going to start happening beyond the touching, but I was young and didn't understand what. My granny's best friend, Linda, moved downstairs. It was like my mom moved down there as well. After being sick, she was down there all day and she started drinking. Every day when we came home from school for lunch, mother was at her friends' house; my step dad would find his way upstairs. I didn't think he had a job. They were drinking beer in the middle of the day, and us kids had to get our own food and go back to school. When we got home and I was alone, he was very busy with his hands feeling me up and saying, "Mmm." I was a young girl and didn't know he was a dog. He would put his hands down into my clothes and feel me. One day, mom and her friend were buzzed when we came home. He made sure they would be drunk and asleep. He sent my brothers and sisters to the store. I was left alone so he could have his way with me. He called it a game; that is why he was watching me all the time. This time I felt like, what do I do? I was so scared, no one ever told me about this. It felt wrong and I was scared. He told me he would kill me if I told, and I didn't know what to do. He would rub what he called his tool on my legs and between them. It would make me wet, he made sounds and his eyes rolled up in his head. I feel so dirty just writing this, but it must be told. After five and a half years, I was talking to one of my friends', Jeana, she told me I needed to tell someone what was going on. This is when I knew I was a broken girl. I told him I was going to tell and he told me he would kill my mom. He continued to watch me and I continued being scared. He'd rub his tool between my legs and said, "Yes, you're ready for this." He tried to push up inside of me, it began to hurt. I cried, and once again, something came out of him and it was wet and sticky. I didn't know what that was that came out of him, I just felt nasty. No one ever had a talk about sex with me, they didn't even teach it in school. He told me to go wash it off; I would go back to school. He did this every school day and mom never came upstairs, she trusted him. Sometimes I'd be late going back to school. Mom didn't think about him ever doing this to me. I began to wonder if she found out, would she hate me? One day, he and mom got into it, they were yelling, I didn't know what they were fussing about, but it was bad. She told him to get out. I felt she would tell me to get out too, because maybe he told her he had wet my bottom up many times. But I was wrong, it was about her friend, he had sex with her when they were drunk. Mom had passed out before her that day. I felt so relieved, because mom wasn't saying "get out" to me. She didn't know what he had done to me, and I'm not going to tell her. Mom was so hurt, but I was free; or so I felt. That man sill watched me when I walked to school. I felt like he might kill me or rape me. My friend Jeana told me about sex and rape. She said he had been raping me. We moved closer to Jeana, but I was afraid to be alone. I was always with someone, I never told my mom; I was ashamed and afraid. Why did this happen to me? I often asked myself. The Creator must be watching this whole thing happen to me. I felt so unloved and so ugly; I had low self-esteem and walked with my head down. Yes, we moved, and I tried to settle into the new neighborhood, but there was something wrong with this picture. No matter what I did, I didn't fit in. The kids called me an oddball, this I didn't understand. I was just trying to be me, whoever I was. I met this lady named Judy; she was the lady who all the kids called grandma, and mom paid her to look after us while she worked. Mom had a full-time day job, but she also had a part time night job. Judy always told all the kids what they should do right. I told her the kids call me an oddball, she said, "Baby, God made you that oddball they call you, and it's for a reason, we all have a purpose in this life, you have to reach out for what's yours." Many laughed at me when I told them what I felt. I later found out it was because they wanted to do some of the things I did, but were too afraid. As I went about my daily business, I didn't trust anyone, and I never liked people in general. These children were mean, and anger grew inside of me for them. One day on the way home from school, children surrounded me and began hitting me and calling me an oddball. They were cussing at me saying, "How come you're not like us, why don't you do what we do, and where did you come from?" We lived on the other side of town, I thought," is that what they were talking about?" I didn't think about me being different, I was just being me. I thought, "How do I act different from them, what were they talking about?" Lord help me, I was an abused child, now these kids are hurting me too. I remembered what Judy said, God made me like he made you and he loves me like he loves you. They beat me down even more. Then my little brother ran and got Judy. She came running and screaming, "Stop hitting her, you nasty little brats." They began to run and Judy said, "Grab the one closest to you; we're going to teach them not to mess with you anymore." So, I grabbed hold to the slowest one. Judy asked, "Did she hit you?" and I said yes. Judy said, "Beat her; she can't fight without her friends." I hit her, Judy said, "harder." For a moment, I think I lost it. I hit that girl with all my might for everything anyone had done to me, even the abuse I suffered. Something stopped me and told me, "You made your point." Judy said, "She'll tell the others and they will see that you're not afraid to fight back." Before I let go of her, I raked my nails across her face just like she did me. I made an ugly mark just like the one I felt bleeding on my face. One by one, I would catch one of them alone. I followed them and I knew where each one lived. Yes, it felt good to beat them up, and they started calling me crazy. I would jump out of the bushes to beat them up. We were still being watched as my brothers and I went to school. After that, they gave us the evil eye, but no one dared to hit us, until Carlisa came to our school. She started kicking ass and taking names of who she thought she could get. Every day she began giving me the evil eye and it was telling me that I was next, because they told her what happened to me when I was jumped. Carlisa said no one's bad except her. Every day she would stare and point her finger at me. One day on my way home, she grabbed some girl and began hitting her. The girl yelled for help, but none of the kids helped her. Carlisa looked at me and yelled, "You're next." I kept walking home, but was ready to fight after I saw how she kicked that girl in the head and dragged her all over the street. I said to myself, "She's not going to do me like that." I told Miss Judy and she said, "You're going to have to fight," then I was ready for her. One day Carlisa began to follow me home. I didn't want my siblings hurt, and I told them to run as fast as they could to get Miss Judy, because she kept us every day while mom worked. Carlisa brought all her friends to come beat me up, that was her motive of operation. One of them grabbed my baby brother and I hit her in the head and she let him go. I yelled, "Run," and it looked like they were chasing us home. We made it to the front of the house. They ran to the front of the house and onto the front of the porch with Judy. I stood my ground. I said, "Come on this is it; you are not going to kick my ass." She said, "You bad, throw the first punch," and I did as hard as I could. Miss Judy said, "Hit her girl, she will never mess with you again." I said, "I was not going to let them make me the mouse again as I hit her." When I hit, her she hit me, I was outside of my body; for a second I, couldn't feel myself. She tried to pick me up, but I weighed more than her and she couldn't lift me. Carlisa's friends began to laugh because she couldn't beat me. I kind of laughed inside, because all the others saw she wasn't as bad or as strong as they thought she was. This day was a total embarrassment for her. At that point, I stopped hitting her; because I saw no need to continue. Carlisa then began to run down the street to her house in tears. All her so-called friends began to cheer me on. I walked up on my porch and closed the door. I didn't look back; I didn't feel like I did so much, however, the other kids felt like I freed them from that bully. After all the beating's I endured from those bully's in my past, I felt good about this. I felt like no one else would fear their bully(s) again. Again, I feel like I'm being watched. We are always being watched. Then I began to watch my watchers. I couldn't go anywhere or do anything without them trying to see what I was doing. People were just nosey, because they wanted what I had or they were trying to keep up, or out do the next person. Some called it paranoia or big brother is watching. If a person does something the government considers against the law, they will be watched and they made it known to that person. As I began to get older, I found that life can come back around and bite you. I say this because, there was nothing a person could hide or keep secret. If you try to be successful in life like get into the movies or music industries, they would dig back in the past to when your mom pushed you from her womb, and that's how much people pay attention to what's going on in your life. Okay, back to my life. At sixteen, I felt like I was the one watching, but I didn't trust anyone and always looked behind me to see who was there. I continued to live my life. I said to myself, "No one wants to know about my life," but I was wrong. I went to look for a job, and this woman told me, because I acted up this past year, they would not help me get a job, as if I committed a murder or something. I was just like every teen, maybe I was a little bad, because I tried to be like them. I tried hard to fit in, because I knew they watched me. I didn't want to be that mouse, but still I was. I couldn't get the job because of some childish thing, but don't we all do things? Why did some folks get away with it and others didn't? Okay, I did get a job, but not the one I wanted. They say it's better than nothing, but that's bull, that means some get pushed into things they don't like. I was never told that my life should go anywhere, so I lived day by day. No one told me there was something I should be doing, like making a life for myself. Many of us never think about it, until you find yourself in a messed-up time in your life. On this job, I met this boy. I began to think about love, something I felt I'd never get. He was a very good looking boy. He and I became that couple in school, and I knew we were being watched. People could be so mean. I was called a whore and many other things, because they wanted to make us break up. When I heard about them gossiping about us, it wasn't anything good. It made feel like I was in the middle of a breakdown, but I wasn't going to let that happen. We went on a date and he felt it was time to take our relationship to another level; we were going to have sex. Something that others have said we have already done, but we had not. Now; I really felt I loved Jim, but it was just puppy love. Boys have sex with girls because they are silly in love, or think they are. Jim was much older than I. I didn't know that he bet the other boys in school that he would be my first. This would be real sex, not what my step-dad did. Up until then, I tried not to let others know what I was doing, but they found out anyway. After it happened, everyone in school knew about it. Jim told them, that dog; they even told my boss in the after-school program where I worked. Jim made a bet I would have sex with him, but I didn't know I would lose my job, until he told everyone what happened. I was hurt, but so in love. My boss told me I could no longer work in close quarters with Jim, I felt like a total whore. I have only had one boyfriend, and that was Jim. I now know that my relationship with Jim was based on a bet. I was heartbroken when I found out. I felt like I loved him, but that was just puppy love, but you don't know it if you think it's real. I wasn't going to let this stop me. People were laughing and talking about me. I cried when I got home, but I wouldn't let them see me. One day I got called into the office, my boss fired me because I told her to just butt out of my life. This was an after-school program, and I started the job before Jim, and I got let go. She told my mom that it had something to do with Jim. That wasn't my mom's business, that old battle axe. I couldn't get around this. I was mad and I called her and let her have it, it wasn't her place to tell my mom anything, that old battle axe. Jim's family moved away and I never saw him again. After he started all of this, I was so mad and now he's gone and I still must live here. I began having pains and feeling sick, I thought my nerves were bad because I was upset. Weeks went by and I didn't see my period, I counted back and said, "No I can't be"! Yes, I was with child and my mom was going to kill me. Now I really feel dirty. I'm always thinking about that nasty man, my step-dad. He had his way with me and how he played me. I began to get sick, but something was wrong. I could feel something tearing my insides out. I was in so much pain, but I couldn't tell mom. I went to my best friends' house and cried for help. She hid me inside her bedroom, we had to go to the hospital; but I didn't right then, until I saw blood. We were going into summer break and I missed the last day of school and the tests were over. My mom knew I was over there. She told me they called her to come back to work, so she wasn't home when this happened. I went back to the house. I went into the bathroom and the baby came out of me into the toilet. I called our family doctor, and I told him what happened. The doctor told me to go to the hospital immediately. Jim had left and I felt more broken. I told the nurses my friend was my mom, we pulled it off and they never questioned her. I got checked out and they let me go, I didn't even have to stay. They told me they removed the rest of it and I should go home and rest. I didn't know if that was right or wrong, I was just glad it was over. The Doctor said no sex for six weeks. I said, "no, never again," but what did I know, I was just a silly teen. No one knew I had a miscarriage, and no one would ever find out. I stayed at her house that night. I could stay with my friend Jeana anytime. My mother never worried about me because Jeana's house was right around the corner. My moms' new boyfriend liked to hit her, but he wouldn't hit me or her when I was with her. While I was away from home, my new step-dad was abusing everyone. He would beat my siblings all the time and mom wouldn't say anything, he was beating her too. He woke us up one night because someone left a bowl in the sink; we all got a beating because we didn't know who did it. My mother and her boyfriend were always yelling and fighting, and my mother would always lose. I hated him so bad. I said to myself, "if he hits me one more time, I will kill him." He came at me one day when mom was at work, I hit him so hard with something and hoped that it killed him, but he was knocked out. It felt good to me and I did this for all of us. I ran to my friends' house and wouldn't go back home for days. Before I left, I told my brothers and sisters to go to the playground until mom got home. I think mom didn't say anything because she knew he would beat me if he got his hands on me, so I hid. My mother told me to come back home, and she promised me that he wasn't going to hit me anymore, because she put him out of her house. I went back home, and summer was just about over, and it was time for me to go back to school. My friends were asking me how my summer was, I told them nothing happened. They watched me to see what I would say, I said nothing. My friend Jeana would not tell a soul. I could always count on her. I met a new girl in my class, her name was Tangee, and she was crazy, fun to be with, and she always made us laugh. She would disrupt class with jokes and get sent to the Dean's office. She would ask questions that were very private. I wasn't going to tell her my life story. She seemed to like school and it was fun to her. One night, she asked me to go with her to a party on the other side of town. I said, "Mrs. Wilson (mom) won't let me go to parties." Tangee said, "I'll ask her." Mom said to Tangee, "I don't know you, no she can't go," but for some reason, the next day she changed her mind. I guess mom thought she would trust me. I was getting older and needed to be around teens like me. Okay, I didn't know what to think about this party. Jeana said she was going too. We got to the party and some of our classmates were there too. It was all right, boys tried to dance with me, they said, "Mouse is here," that's what they called me. They asked me if I could dance and I began to show them my moves. This was the first time I danced in front of people. Everyone wanted to dance with me, as they saw how good I could do it. The girls were looking too. Mouse can move I could hear some of them say bad things, but I just kept on dancing. I wouldn't let the boys dance too close to me, and there was absolutely no slow dancing. I wouldn't let them get close to me; it felt like I did when I was molested by my step-dad. It messed my mind up, but then I wanted to fit in; but no one was going to grind on me. It looked like sex on the dance floor with your clothes on. The next day at school, word came back to us that we were getting beat up by this gang called War Lords, because we were dancing with their boyfriends. But it was just dancing, and then I heard they said, "Mouse not you," because I was the only one who didn't slow dance with the girls' boyfriends. After I was told this, I took the messages back and forth. There were so many gangs in my school. I didn't belong to any of them, but they had me carrying the messages. Then one day Tangee said, "Let's go for a walk." We began to walk, when I saw where she was headed, I said, "Don't go into the War Lords turf, they are not playing with you; they are going to get you." She felt like she was bad and we continued to walk in that direction. Tangees' two sisters met us. We walked and talked; I looked up the street and saw the War Lords were in front of us. I said we were in too deep and let's go north, the other way, and they would not follow; but Tangee wanted to keep going in like she was bad. I stopped dead in my tracks and I was telling them to turn north into the other turn. At that point, they came behind us and we were in the middle of a circle of forty to fifty girls. I said, "I hope you can run, because there's going to be a fight and we are outnumbered." Some of them went to our school. Tangee didn't look scared, she was ready to fight, why didn't she listen to me and go the other way? Big Sue said, "Let the Mouse go." My heart fell to my feet, and I started to walk. Then she said, "We want these girls." Tangee said, "Stay with us Mouse," but I felt I could go for help. They let me go because my Grandpa lived in the War Lords projects, and I went there every weekend. All the kids loved grandpa there. He gave them candy and toys. When Big Sue said let me go, I ran home as fast as I could. When I got home, I told mom and she called the police. They took a beating, but no one was seriously hurt, just bruised and a few black eyes. They were mad at me because I left them. When help arrived, the gang ran, they did not fight them back, so they didn't get stomped and kicked. I felt bad, now they didn't want to talk to me or listen to me. All they had to do was turn around, the gang wanted them. Should I have taken a beating for one of them, they wouldn't for me; only Jeana was that kind of friend. From that day on, Tangee wouldn't talk to me. I still had my friend Jeana. I told her that I told Tangee not to go there, and she went anyway and got beat up. After that, Tangee gave me nasty looks and wouldn't talk to me anymore. Mom said she wasn't my friend anyway. After the party, the boys tried to hit on me saying, I could do my best moves under one of them, so I played and flirted with a lot of them, that's how I got my reputation. I began living a nasty little life. I wanted someone to love me, but I didn't know how to get it. What my step-dad did to me, just made me mess my life up. If they didn't love me, they would love it. I became very promiscuous. I felt like my step-dad destroyed me at such a young age, so I started acting like it. My mom was going through some hard times. I went to live with grandma and papa, living there was okay, but I didn't see my brothers and sisters that much. In a short period, mom pulled it all together and found a new home. Oh, my God, this street was crazy, all those people in and out of buildings all night long. I didn't know about drugs then, so maybe that's what was going on. I was afraid all the time, and they watched everything we did. It was just us kids, while mom worked late, I would feed the kids and put them to bed before she got home. I would wait up for her, my mom worked so hard. She told us we were going to do better, and we will be moving soon, and we did; two weeks after she said that. This time we moved into a nicer place and I still went to the same school. Afterwards, boys began hitting on me and I became a flirt. I began meeting the kids in our new building. This is when mom met someone named Mr. Bob. He was just what the doctor ordered for mom. She was very happy and he was good to all of us. He moved in and changed our home. He brought all new furniture, new window treatments, the works; we had our own beds, three in the girls' room and three in the boys' room. For the first time, we had food, more than mom could put in the house. Until now, she had to pay the bills all by herself, but Mr. Bob made it good and easier for her. The only thing was, he liked to party. At first it seemed all right, but the third floor started to party a bit more. Mr. Bob was a good cook, so he sold what he cooked to them. They were all drunk upstairs, and we never saw the people, they would use the back way to go upstairs; however, we could hear the parties. These parties became so big, that they would put all the kids in one apartment; ours. I was the oldest, so I was in charge of watching twenty kids in a three-bedroom apartment. We had fun, but I wouldn't let them tear up the place, because I loved the way it looked. We were fed takeout food, or sometimes Mr. Bob would cook and we ate it all up. These parties would last all night. As it got late, I would make the kids go to sleep. The kids were everywhere, but I managed to find a spot on my own bed. It was morning, and slowly they would leave. Mr. Bob and mom would go into their room after it was over. The parties were every weekend. I heard them say they were swingers, at the time; I didn't know what that meant. I asked someone and when they told me, I thought, "Wow what the heck is that, what are they doing?" They would never let me know. By now I was growing very tired of this. Then one night they began to fight at the party. I became very afraid for mom. I heard yelling and screaming. I tried to keep the kids inside the apartment, I wanted them to feel safe, but I didn't know what was going on. Just when I thought the fight was over, mom and Mr. Bob came into the apartment; and he beat my mom. She was crying and went inside their bedroom, and he went too. From then on, he would beat my mom up. She wouldn't swing with the swingers, and this made him mad. She would go to work with black eyes, or bites on her arms and face. He acted like he wanted to take away her good looks. I remember one time he had us go outside, and he locked the door so we couldn't get in. We were outside crying. We heard glass breaking and things falling, Mr. Bob was breaking up everything inside the apartment. We knew she was trying to run from him because her screams came from different rooms. We cried so hard that day, we wanted to kill him. We sat outside on the steps and cried as hard as we could. We no longer wanted him to stay with us. Poor mom, she started not to care about herself. She would no longer go to the parties. Mr. Bob wanted to use her for his own benefit. Then he began to beat me and my brothers and sisters. Once again, I found myself saying, "If he ever hits me again, I'm going to kill him." I was a child and this hurt me so bad. One day, I think it was my turn; he hit mom and she couldn't go to work. Then he began to yell at me. Mom had some wine bottles from around the world, and the next thing I knew; my brother stabbed him in the back with scissors. He came at me and I hit him so hard, he fell back onto the floor, I said, "Oh no I killed him!" He was just knocked out and bleeding from the scissors my brother stabbed him with. I ran as I saw him get up and come after me. Mom and the kids began to hit him with anything they could find. He looked at us and went out the door. We thought that was the last time we'd ever see him, but I was wrong. Mom threw the TV out the window at him. He wanted all the things he brought for us back, and we wanted to give them to him. Mom said, "Before I let you beat me again, I'll give it all up." The next day mom looked for a new house and said we would soon move again. We moved a lot, always trying to run away from issues. When Mr. Bob found out we were moving, he began knocking on the door bugging mom and wanted her to take him back. He would get loud. We lived on the third floor, and we would begin throwing things at him out of the window. He would leave; then he would come back another time. One day mom was going to be honored on her job. She was waiting for her ride, and when they didn't come, she began to walk. About a half hour later, she came running down the street. When she left, she was dressed in all white, but now, she was covered in mud from her head to her toes and her mouth was bleeding. Mr. Bob had knocked all my mom's front teeth out, top and bottom. He must have kicked them out. We grabbed her and we all cried and told her we would really hurt him if he ever came back to our house. Moms' face was swollen. We washed her face and got her some clothes to wear. Anger filled all of us; we hoped he wouldn't ever come back, because we would have been locked up. Okay, this is just what the doctor ordered; this was so I could free myself from all that mayhem going on in my little life. Why am I the one? What can this life mean to me; right now, I'm so confused. Am I living so people can mistreat me and my family? Folks always told me that I'm blessed, after this; I wonder. I later found out people witnessed this happen, and no one tried to stop it, what if that was their mom, what would they do? Like I said earlier, someone watched us all the time. You are known by the friends you keep, the car you drive and what size you are, you're always under surveillance. About six months after, I met who would be the father of my children. Mom met him and she didn't like him. I didn't listen to her because I felt that she didn't pick a good man, but I knew what I was doing. Now as I began to be around him, I found out he didn't know half of what I knew. I found myself trying to help him understand some things. He couldn't read, and I felt it was my duty to teach him. Mom said he was dumb as a box of rice, whatever that meant. He did have something good about him; he was very kind to me. A gentle type of person, he opened doors for me, bought me lunch, flowers, and candy. This was the man I'd be with for the rest of my life. We dated for two years, and what I really liked about him is he never asked or talked about sex. The boys I went to school with, that's all they ever wanted to talk about, and I was not going to rack up more sexual partners, if you know what I mean. I already had my reputation.

CHAPTER TWO – SHE DIDN'T LIKE HIM

My best friend Jeana said he must be gay; I got mad and yelled at her, "Is that all you think about?" She didn't like him and mom didn't like him either. I asked Jeana, "Would you like someone treating you like a piece of meat or and an object they can use?" All I knew is he was good to me. Mom recovered from what Mr. Bob had done to her, and began to move on with her life. She went to the Dentist and got new dentures too, but she became very depressed and cried a lot. She was always afraid that if she met someone, he would treat her the same way. She couldn't bring herself to date; this went on for nine years. Now let's go back to my life. After two years of dating, my boyfriend said he felt it was time for us to have sex. I told him we weren't married and I didn't want children out of wedlock. But that soon flew out the window. You see, his older brother came to our town and began telling him things. I wanted to believe I was grown up, but it was the blind leading the blind. He didn't know what sex was either. When mom went to work, I asked him to come by. She had to go back to working two jobs to make ends meet. When I put the younger kids to sleep, my boyfriend and I would go at it. I knew more about sex than him, or so he said I did. It wasn't bad, but after that, it was all he wanted to do every time we saw each other. One day, he wanted to have sex with no protection, and I said no, we don't need children right now. He told me about a story his doctor back home said, regarding him not being able to father children.

Like a fool, I was naïve and fell for it. One month later I missed my cycle and two more weeks I was with child. I told him we need to find our own place, because I couldn't tell my mom I messed up. He found a room and we left. I was gone for two weeks and I didn't think mom would worry about me, but Jeana told me mother was asking her about me, thinking she knew where I was. Then I called mom and told her why I left. She said she thought as much and told me to get home, but I wanted to stay with him. He started abusing me and saying this is not what he wanted. He would cuss at me and all I did was cry. When I was about five months pregnant, he hit me. My whole world fell apart that day. I saw my mom go through this. He would quickly make up, which made me feel good. We called mom one cold December night and told her it's time. Mother met us at the hospital and my labor was fast, our son was born. Now I thought our life would be good, but he became mean, always cussing, and complaining about everything. I wanted to walk out, but I didn't want to take care of this child by myself and end up like mom. Then he started hitting me, just like what happened to mom. I couldn't tell her, because she told me this could happen. I didn't want to hear her say I told you so, therefore, I just took it. I got a full-time job because he complained about he couldn't make ends meet. Although I was working, he still came up short. I would pay the bills when he didn't. He started buying brand new clothes and I didn't have money for myself. I was mom all over again.

I told myself I would never be her, oh my God; what am I going to do? I tried to talk to him about how he should pay the bills, and the next day I had to work with a black eye. I wore sunglasses and my co-workers new something was wrong; there was no sunlight that day. The next weekend my lip was busted. I was mad and not wanting to be with him anymore, but we would make up. Like I said, I didn't want to take care of my child alone, but he wasn't much of a father. One night he wanted to have sex. I said no, because the doctor told me no sex for six weeks after giving birth to my son. We began to fight and he forced himself on me. I cried as he took it, and this made me come to the realization that I had to leave; but I didn't have the money. I was trying to keep the bills caught up in the house, that kept me broke and he knew it. My clothes were old and my shoes were run over. I was broke with no money and had no place to go. I could not go to moms'; she had enough trying to take care of the kids and her own bills. I continued to work and now my checks went into an account with both our names on it. I thought to myself, "I will stop paying most of the bills, the money will build up and then I would leave." When he started seeing the money building up, he wondered what was going on. When I said, we spend too much and we should try to save more, he punched me so hard I saw stars. While lying on the floor, I felt something move inside of me. Everything was all messed up. I never thought about that night he forced me to have sex with him, and once again I was with child. I went to the doctor with a black eye. He asked what happened; I said I walked into a door. He said, yes; don't walk into it anymore. Then he said you are going to have a baby. I wanted to scream. I went home and told him, and he hit me repeatedly. All I could do was lie on the floor and cry. Now I knew I couldn't go to moms'. I tried to get someone to help me, but there was no one. I stayed and took the abuse. One day he went out the door and got in the car. I ran after him. He let the window down and yelled and cussed at me. When he rolled the window up, my sleeve got caught in the window. Then he took off, he began to drag me along. I screamed, "I'm stuck to the car." I got pulled about two car lengths. He finally stopped and rolled the window down. When I got my sleeve out the window, he rolled the window back up and took off. He didn't even try to see if I was all right, and I was carrying his child. He tried to make me loose the baby, but I didn't. After the beating and dragging, my mother came to see me. She got mad at me and told me I didn't have to live like that. I was bruised, I had a black eye and my knees were all scraped up. I checked our account and there was a lot of money in it. I took some money out, only what had come from my checks and I moved away from him. He found out where I was and begged me to come back to him, but I needed to make it on my own and away from him. Our child had begun to be afraid of him too. I didn't want to be like mom. He promised he wouldn't hit me anymore, and we began to date again, to make sure this is what he and I wanted. It was six months; he became very nice to me. He was taking me places and doing all kind of things for me and his son. I began to get big and close to having the baby, the child that was conceived by him forcing himself on me after I told him no. I felt that I needed to give him a second chance, and I was pressured into giving him that chance. When I came home, I told him to move his things into my place and let his place go. We had a little girl; she was so beautiful to me. I felt I would settle into my life. Time went on; we eventually got married and had a total of four children. As life, would have it, that old devil would rear his head again. I liked the place where I moved too. I knew people were watching me, but I felt it was good, because my husband was a crazy man, and no one would mess with us. Now that he moved in, I didn't want them in my business. One girl watched every time my husband went to work. She was always outside her door. Every time he walked out, she made sure he saw her as she yelled, "Hi." I never thought about him cheating, but I was so blind. He began leaving a lot after work. I knew everyone needed a little space, so I didn't say anything, but I began to watch what was going on. Miss Lady would come in front of my house and walk back and forth. This started happening more often as I continued to watch what was going on. I couldn't believe after all we were going through, all the hell with him, he's now cheating on me. I got mad. He started putting his change of clothes in his car and he spent more hours away from home. My family members would come and tell me what they saw. I had to talk to him about this. I told him, "If that's where you want to be, you need to go there." He just looked at me and walked out the door. I saw that old look in his eyes, the look he used to have when he hit me. He was gone for three days, and then he came back. I wanted to say something to him, but I was afraid and I didn't want him to hit me anymore. He came and went as he pleased. I had children to take care of, and that's what I did. I took care of the household. I started a little business out of my home, so I didn't need a babysitter. He bought me a sewing machine. I started making clothes for people, and it was going well. People started telling others, and my business was growing and getting better. When he saw that I was doing so well, he started his old tricks of not paying the bills. I started doing the same thing I did in the past, but this time I had a backup. I began paying the bills that were in my name, and I stopped paying the bills that were in his name. I was about to move away again, then my granny told me to stay, because the kids need to stay in one place and all that moving was not good for young children. He went on doing whatever he wanted and I continued to take care of my kids. One day he told me that he got a promotion at work and he was going to be the night shift manager. He said he could get me a job and we could work together, and I wouldn't have to make clothes anymore. This would be more money for the both of us, and mom would keep the kids at night. I decided to work the night shift with him. Well, I found out he handpicked the staff for the night crew from the day shift. He kept me from working around everyone else, and told me he didn't want anyone to mess with me. I liked working alone anyway, it made me work faster. They trusted him; he had they keys and ran the shift well. When work ended, everyone was so nice and said goodbye with a smile. I would say to him; they are so nice; he would just look at me and roll his eyes. One night I couldn't get my machine to work. I started to look for him. The plant was big and I didn't know my way around. I was lost in this huge plant, I said to myself, "Turn around and go back the way you came." My turn around took me to a place where people were talking and laughing. When I got there, I asked where is the manager and no one knew. At that point I decided to walk down the hallway. There was a door to a room labeled, "Managers Office." I opened the door, and to my surprise, he had one of the female co-workers bent over his desk. I lost my mind. I didn't know what I was throwing, but I think it was some office supplies. I hit them both and he was hitting me too. She ran around the office screaming as I hit her. Someone heard the commotion and called his boss. The police were called and I was told I wasn't going to jail. My employer told me they were not going to let me work there anymore, and for me to go home. I left, got my children, and went home. He stayed and worked the rest of that night. When he came home he started hitting me, but this time I fought back, and I wanted him to leave. This carried on until almost morning. I went into one bedroom, locked me and kids inside and went to sleep. After that, I could never trust him again. He didn't leave, but swore he would be true to me from that point on; and I didn't mention anything about it ever again. As time went by I knew I had to look for work. I always wanted to work with children. I got a job driving school buses. My husband began to drink; this is something he had never done before. When he drank, he became very nasty. A lot of times I just tried to stay out of his way. We had new neighbors who were from the south. I couldn't understand some of the words they would say. Among the new neighbors was this man, there was something strange about him; he looked at me all the time. When I walked out my door he would often come out. He would scare me and with that old evil laugh. He was a very handsome man, but strange. One day as we passed, he grabbed and pulled me close to him and planted a kiss on my mouth. I pulled away and told him not to ever do that again. He laughed that evil way he always did. The way the house was made, you couldn't see someone until they walked out of the bushes. He would come out every day. I tried to leave a little late, but he was still there, no matter what time; he would just be there. His wife didn't see what was going on, or anyone else, that's why he could keep messing with me every day. One day I told him to stop looking at me and messing with me. He said he wanted me and he had never been turned down. He said, "I watch you and him, and you're not satisfied, anyway, I hear you and him." He would hear me and my husband yelling and fighting upstairs. He said, "I know there's no happiness there." It was true, there was no happiness, but that was none of his business. He made me think about emotions, I had hidden inside of me for a while. Then he began to give me little gifts. He would always tell me how good I looked, and I started to like it. He was paying attention to me when no one else did, and I got sucked in. I started to talk to him, and slowly I began to like him as a friend. It was not as bad as I felt in the beginning. This man was trying to make me love him, so that I wouldn't or couldn't say no to him anymore. The gifts were getting more expensive. He would give me back all the money I paid his wife to keep my kids, he even added more money to it. Why did I have this greed inside of me, or was it because another man was paying attention to me. He treated me like I always wanted to be treated, I just wanted to be wined and dined. My husband wouldn't do it. I always wanted to be treated like that. One day he asked to take me to lunch, I didn't go because I thought about how I felt when my hubby messed up and cheated on me. His wife, Lola, would kill me for having an adulterous affair with her man. He started coming to my job and stalking me, to a point I started feeling afraid. I asked him why. He said, "I love you, and I know you feel something for me, you can't say no, and I'll make sure you don't." Then he said, "Meet me after work and let's talk more about it." I did like him, a lot. What was I going to do? We went to lunch and later we rented a room. It's like I couldn't say no after talking with him about his problems. Deep inside I wanted him, or anyone who would pay attention to me. He told me I was beautiful, I didn't want to give in. I felt like I was under a spell. I didn't care who was watching me at that time. That was the first time I felt I was making love. The way he handled me was surprising. He was very gentle and passionate. When it was over, I began to cry, not because I messed up, these were happy tears. I had let my emotions die and he made everything I felt come back alive. Why didn't I find someone like him years ago, then he began to cry, I said, "I'm sorry." He told me why he cried, cancer was going to take his life and the Doctor didn't give him very much time. We stayed out late just talking and wondering what's going to be said when we get home. He went home first. I left and went to moms to get the kids. When I got home, hubby wasn't there anyway, so the kid's and I got ready for bed. This time I could hear them yelling and her crying downstairs. I lived upstairs and I felt very bad, why did I ever give in to him? The next day I tried to leave before he came out, but he was there. "I love you," were the words I didn't want to hear. Tears filled his eyes as I told him I had to leave him alone. We didn't see each other after that, maybe in passing. When I did see him, he began to look sick. A few months went by and they moved. Lola told me where they were moving, and that he told her what happened between us. I felt so bad, and I told her I was sorry, but my words couldn't help how she felt. She wanted me to know, because he asked her to tell me before he passed. She knew that he would be dead soon and she wanted to give him his last wish. Within a few days, he died. Tears filled my eyes as I tried to comfort her. He left her with six children and slowly we became friends after his passing. As time went by she said, "Don't feel bad you weren't the only one he had been with." She had been through years of abuse too. Love sank like a stone just thinking about him and how he had treated her and the kids. By now driving school buses was getting hard, the kids were bad and they gave me a route on the wild side of town. The route I was given was for the kids who had defiant and rebellious problems. They called it "detention run." They had a teacher who rode in the back of the bus to stop anything that was about to happen, or call for help if things really got out of hand. Mr. Mitts was his name. Like I said, someone was always watching me, and he was. I watched him work with them while God was watching all of us. I needed to move away from the past situations that continue to haunt me here. I moved to the other side of town. My husband was still with us, but we didn't have much to say to each other; which was fine with me. Little did I know there was going to be another kind of attack on the way. My job hired a whole new crew of people, and some of them were nasty. I went into the office one day, and all eyes were on me, I said to myself, "Why?" I took a bath, I fixed my hair, and I put on clean clothes; I didn't understand what the problem was. There was this person named Barb, she was the ring leader. She was the bitch from hell. I was told so many bad things about that woman, and I was about to learn for myself. Everyone talked about her party's and orgies. I was asked to come to one of them, I said, "No thanks, I don't hang out with those kinds of people." Well, this started it. Word got back to her about me calling her, "Those people." She acted like a child and wanted to get back at me for saying that. She began to watch everything I did. She asked people about my life and she began insulting me about what happened in my past. She had a lot of people on her side; they did things as favors for her. I started feeling like she was Carlisa all over again. I would get home and someone would continuously call my house and when I answered the phone they would just hang up. I have never had this happen to me before. I thought to myself who could be doing this? I've always been a person who has kept to myself. I knew it had to be someone from the job. This is the first time in a while that I have had anyone mess with me like this. One day, I dropped my hubby off and drove to my job; it was on the other side of the same work park. The bus drivers were always in the office that faced the front part of the building, where my husband was working. Barb and her people watched us every day as we parted. She thought she knew what was going on in my life. I had no reason to change my routine and continued to live each day. I just wanted to have a normal life and for my kids to grow up happy, whatever that meant. My husband and I would still fight, in fact we used to get into the car and drive away from the house to fight. I would always lose. We had a talk with the doctor about disrupting our children's growth. The Doctor didn't want us to mess their heads up any worse than they already were. After his advice, we would go on long rides to keep from fighting in front of the kids. When hubby was tired of arguing, we would go home. I would go to work and all eyes would be on me, like I should be feeling a certain kind of way, but what was it? I would pull into the bus loop every day and go into the bathroom. All my identification was inside my purse, and I have never had any problems with people touching my things. My paychecks were always deposited into my checking account, and I would always pay my bills on time. There was a large amount of money in the account. I got my statements every week, and for a month, someone was taking money out. I looked for my checkbook and couldn't find it. I went to the bank and told them I was missing money and someone was forging my checks. The bank did an investigation and credited the money back into my account. I later found out Barbs' daughter, who worked at the bank; was cashing them for her. I said, "I'll let the law take care of this." I wanted to put my foot up her behind, but I refrained from doing anything because I knew she would get her just due in the end. I still went to work and said nothing to her. She acted like I didn't know about what she had done with her daughter, who was a spoiled brat. This lady named Millie told me Barb was a piece of work. Millie's kids and friends knew Barb knew things about all of them; she used that information to blackmail them. They did whatever she told them to do. A few weeks went by without any of Barb's harassment. I stopped to get gas before I went to work, because that was one less thing I had to worry about. It was Friday and time to punch out. I hopped into the car and drove off, then the car cut off in the middle of the road, and I knew I had just filled my car with gas before I came to work. Barb drove slowly pass me and laughed. I looked at the gauge and the car was empty. She had someone steal gas out of my car, and she thought it was funny. I called my husband and told him what happened, and he went and got gas for my car. I made sure to put a locked gas cap on my car after that incident. I told Millie on Monday morning, and she said she thinks it was Barb's friend, one of the bus attendants who stole my gas. I heard them talking about it. I started watching them just like they were watching me. Sneaking around gave me more information than waiting for someone to tell me. I would walk up on them talking, and they stopped talking when they saw me. I started to say things like, "I'm going to get whoever is messing with me. I called the phone company and they traced the calls, and I found out who the co-worker was calling me and hanging up. The telephone company shut off her phone immediately because she was harassing me on my home phone. That Friday evening, I drank a Pepsi. When I woke up that Saturday morning, it felt like I had been drinking alcohol or someone had put something in my Pepsi. I looked around and saw hair everywhere. I put my hand on my head and some of my hair had been cut off. How could I have not felt that someone was cutting my hair? I must have drunk something strong to make me sleep so hard. How could I tell anyone that someone came into my house and cut some of my hair off, who would believe me? That was the weekend when I was alone. I changed the locks on my doors. On Monday, I came into work with less hair, but I cut it even to make it look better. They were standing around the time clock when I walked in, and someone said, "Nice haircut," and everyone started laughing. They conjured up other things. In the meantime, they continued to throw their parties, and I would hear so many stories. One girl found out her man was hanging out there spending all his money, and by the time he got home he had spent his whole paycheck. Barb made sure the people who came paid for everything, which included food, drinks, and sex. One day, the lady went there looking for her man. She saw his car parked outside, and someone at the door said he was not there; however, she pushed her way into the house. Once inside, she saw her man dancing and having fun. She ran up to him and they began to fight. People tried to pull them apart. They were told to leave; Barb didn't want the police there. There were to many illegal things going on inside, all of them might go to jail, and they had to leave. Millie had already told me about everything that went on there.

CHAPTER THREE – I WANTED TO PULL MY LIFE AWAY

I wanted to pull my life away from the things that happened. I needed to look for a new job. I wanted to leave that job so bad, but I needed the money to take care of my children. I couldn't rely on my husband; I had to make sure we could live. I wanted to tell someone what happened, but who would believe me? They did so many things; I sometimes felt I was crazy. I had an interview and I went to it. It seemed like a very good job, but it was inside and I would have to change a lot of things. As I drove, my whole muffler system dropped to the ground. Later I was told the clamps had somehow fallen off; I knew that couldn't just happen. I saw Barb drive passed me laughing. I knew they had done this to me again. I had to call my husband once again; and we had to fix the car. He didn't believe me when I told him about the other incidents, so I kept this one to myself. Millie told me Barb said she would do all kinds of things to keep me from having anything, by causing me to have to spend money and never being able to save. How could I make them leave me alone? I said I was going to buy a gun, and I eventually did. I didn't know if I would use it or not, but I was mad enough to use it. I felt kind of crazy, they're watching me and I'm watching them, this was sick. At this point I started to load my gun and I drove towards them. I was going to go in there and kill Barb and all her friends. Then I pictured my children with a dad who didn't love them. I put the gun on the seat, started my car and drove away from that place. I wanted to end it, but I loved my kids and I could not have anyone else raise them, except me. I met a lady at church and she helped me get a job. She worked at that place for years, and within days I got an interview. It went well and I got the job. Around that time my son was about fourteen. His voice was deep and he started to get phone calls from girls. My son would stay on the phone for hours, I said, "He's trying to date some girl." I let him talk and plan his little meeting. They had not met, and I asked him one day where did he meet her. He said she just called one day and they began to talk. She told him she saw him every day, and he said it must be some girl from school, but she had not made herself known. Every day she'd call and they would talk for hours. One day he said he was going to the store to meet her. He was gone for a while, and when he came home sad. He said she didn't show up, he waited for her to call and she didn't. Then Millie called and told me, "I'm going to put you on three way, don't say a word, and just listen." The phone rang and it was Barb. Millie started asking her what happened on the date. Barb started laughing and said her son showed up. She thought she was talking to my hubby on the phone. My son was supposed to be my hubby when he went to the store, because she wanted to do anything to hurt me. She didn't have to give my hubby any help; she didn't do her homework well enough. If she had, she would have known this marriage was already in hell. She should have tried something that would really hurt me. I didn't want to hear anymore and I hung up. I called Barb back and told her, "I heard you want my hubby, you're only one of many, be my guest, but you will go to jail if you call my teenage son again." Sometimes I wanted to scream and yell to the top of my voice. After I hung up, I called Millie and thanked her for the three-way call. Why have all these things happened to me, then I cried until I couldn't cry anymore. I asked God why, but I didn't get an answer. I looked at others' lives and they seemed so happy, but were they happy? I never knew someone could hate that much. I didn't want to hear anymore, but Millie said there were more things. I didn't want to know and said some other time; I had to get ready for my new job. I walked into the new place on Monday; I wasn't met with a kind face. The lady I had to report too was not nice; she had a chip on her shoulder. She told me her friend should have my job, she asked me how did I rate and who did I know. I just smiled and said nothing, because this was going to pay me a lot of money. I will have enough to take care of my children and walk away from that loveless marriage. I felt her eyes on me all the time, waiting for me to make one mistake so she could send me packing. The job was watching children who had behavior problems. All I had to do was walk the halls every ten minutes and make sure the children were in their bed and not messing with each other. I wasn't told there were sex offenders among the children. Some nights, the bigger boys were raping the little ones. This made me sick inside. If they have that kind of problem, they shouldn't all be in one big room; but they were. Why can't I just do what I'm told and go home? At lunch time, I would go to the basement to do the laundry. One day I noticed the back door was opened. I looked out and saw a car pulling away fast. When I went back upstairs, I wasn't sure what to say. I called the night manager and reported the door was open. I worked until my shift was done and went home. The next day I got a call as I got my children off to school. They wanted to ask me about some stealing going on at work. They said food and milk were being stolen. I told the lady who didn't like me, that I reported the open back door and the car that drove away fast. She said the door wasn't open and I must have done that. I knew then she was going to give my job to her friend. She was setting me up. She left money in the drawer to see if I would take it, and I didn't. She didn't like that, and she was going to find a way to get me out. The guy who sat in for me was looking out the window and saw the same car quickly drive away.

She couldn't fire me yet, she didn't know he was there. I worked for a little while longer. She reported that money was taken from her desk. She tried to say I did it, but I wasn't working that night and it made her look stupid. She told me it was time for my evaluation. I read what she wrote about me, and she said I needed to sign it; I did. Shortly afterwards, I was called into the office and told I was fired. The manager said I wrote terrible things about my own job performance, which was not right, but he took her word over mine, because he liked her. Sometimes, people in authority on jobs let you go for the dumbest reason. One of the girls got fired because she never smiled. Maybe her life wasn't happy, should she smile and cheese just to please her co-workers? That lady wrote all kinds of things that were bad, and she said I couldn't do my job. I hated working there and so did everyone else I worked with. What a lie, I never talked to anyone there. I didn't write that and sign it. I told the manager I would never come into work if I didn't like it. He gave me two weeks to leave, but I did not go for the two weeks. If they didn't believe me then, they might do some more things. I didn't go back there and I returned to driving school buses. They told me to come back the next day, and they didn't want me to leave anyway. I brought myself a new car and things seem to be going very well. Then I started feeling sick. Every night I got sick and vomited. I remembered messing around with that husband of mine about two months ago, Yes, I was with child…again. This was the fifth one. I was vomiting all over the place and could hardly do my job. That old mean woman fired me. I was sick and she had me sign a paper and said it would help me. It was an evaluation and she put all kinds of bad things about me. I trusted her and signed without reading it. I thought I was just upset, because I was going to have another baby. The baby made me very sick and I had to go on bed rest. This was awful, when I got up; I would throw up. I would be lying down, my husband came in yelling and screaming that I needed to get my butt up, go to work and help him pay some bills.

CHAPTER FOUR-GOING THROUGH THE MOTIONS

I started making clothes again for people. More people began ordering from me, that was good money. I made so many clothes, and in fact, people still ask me to make them clothes till this day. My hubby wanted me to get rid of the child, and I wouldn't. He thought he could make me lose my baby with the things he did to me, but that didn't work. After nine months passed, we had a boy. I couldn't let this happen again. I moved into the other bedroom and put a lock on the door, so he couldn't come in. My clothing business was going well. So many folks wanted outfits. It was overwhelming; I needed help. My neighbors' saw how many people were coming and going with outfits and I was asked questions. I noticed this one girl was looking at that husband of mine. The woman across the street told me I should look at what was going on right under my nose. I knew it had to do with him cheating. He was not going to change for anyone. I didn't want to know anything more about him, but everyone knew what kind of man he was. I got a call from my sister. She was very upset. I went to see what was wrong. When I walked inside the house, she was lying on the floor in her own blood. Once again, her husband had beaten her. Her face was pushed in on one side. I took her to the hospital. The bones in her face were broken; they began to wire it up. I felt I should do more about this. I called the police to file a report. After she was released from the hospital, she asked me to take her home to get clean clothes. When we got to her place and opened the door, we couldn't believe our eyes. Every piece of furniture was cut; he had taken an axe to everything. Nothing in the place was usable. She broke down into tears. I told her I would help her get back on her feet. She stayed with me and my hubby. I got her some clothes to wear and took her places to find a job. After a few weeks, she found a job. She didn't finish high school, but she was lucky to be working. She worked and saved her money. She could get her own place, but her husband found out where she was living. He went there and beat her up. She was afraid to live there. She told the landlord, he put her in one of his places where he couldn't get in. The landlord told her to call the police if he was seen by her or any of the neighbors. He didn't go around there. My sister started dating; and the guy she was seeing was very nice to her. He helped her get things for her house. Still, someone was watching all of that, nothing done, day or night got passed God. The things going on in my sister's life took my mind off things I was going through. One day my oldest son told me his Pops took him to some lady's house; his dad took a bike out and gave it to another little boy. My son was mad because he said his dad didn't buy him one. The other boy must have said something to him, because he took care of them, he would leave my children around the corner in his car. Anything could have happened to my children, but all he cared about was himself. My son said he knew where she lived and told me how to get there. I borrowed my next-door neighbors' car. I rolled up on him and saw them with my own two eyes. I got out and said, "So this is where you hang out?" He was hugged up with her. He didn't care that I found him, he just pulled her closer. I went into the car, because when he left, all my money inside my purse was in the car. When I got my purse out the car, I said, "I'll see you when you get home. She asked, "Who are you?" I said, "His wife." She looked at him funny, he hadn't told her. Sometimes people are treated so bad and wonder if they're going to pull through. But they should, because I've been told; life is good and it's too short. All their past and everything that wronged them, they should forget and move on. Sometimes the pain and the scars are deep, but you must forget about it, and I know sounds easier said than done. After all the things, I did for my sister, she turned her back on me too. If a friend does it, it hurts, but my own sister, wow! When she was young, mom put me in charge of them, because I was the oldest. I made sure they were okay; I would have hurt anyone who tried to mess with her. As soon as she got up a little, she gave me her behind to kiss, why and how could she do that? Until this day, I get mad all over again when I think about it. It was over little things, she told lies about me to many of my family members. She thought it was all good, but it wasn't. We came from the same mom, same household, but she chose to be the hateful one. Do we not think that God is watching our lives being played out, but he is watching too? Barb had not gone away; she paid someone to mess with my life. When we were not home, she had someone take my mail. A check was missing and we never got bills. One day, a man I used to work with came to see me at home. He told me he had to get some things off his chest. He said he was dying of cancer and had to tell me those things. He said Barb was seeing the mechanic. She told him to do damage to my cars. When the muffler system fell off the car, he had taken the clamps off the car causing the pipes to fall off. She thought that was the funniest thing. All the gas was sucked out of my car, after I filled the tank that morning. Now I remember seeing him as I got gas. My tires were cut and my car was keyed. She told folks I would not join in with them at her party's and sex games they played. She called me a Queen, and said she planned to unseat/dethrone the Queen. She was the one who stole my checkbook out of my purse and had her daughter cash it. Her daughter got fired for doing so. How can a person be so hateful? When my house keys were missing, they had been inside my home while I was at work. They told someone to pee in my food while they were inside my house. On any given day, my children could have eaten that food. I'm glad Millie told me, how gross. When I got home, I started to smell the food before we ate it. If the food and milk smelled funny, I threw it out and bought more. That same day I changed the locks on my doors to make sure everything was bolted up. I wanted to do something to those people, but I'm glad someone told me what they did before my children and I had eaten anything. I saw them laugh and talk about it thinking we had eaten food that was peed on, but we didn't. The tainted food was all gone, they made me spend extra money, but safety came first. I didn't hang with these folks, I didn't believe in the things they did or said. All of this meant nothing to Barb; my pain was funny to her and the rest of them. Back to the guy who was confessing. My heart went out to this man, because he was living the last days of his life. I felt so bad for him, but he said, "Don't feel bad, I am ready and I'm glad I didn't take this with me." He said he just wanted to tell me what was done and for me to know she hated me. Then he said, "Now maybe some of the things that happened are now clear to you, and you know who did them." Yes, now I know, but what was I to do with this information? Should I call the police, some of the events happened more than a year ago, I had to let Barb know I knew what kind of non-human she really was. Why wasn't I an evil or manipulating kind of person like her? Why can't I feel good when I tear up someone else's property? That was one of the reasons she didn't like me, she felt I was better than her. She should have spent time trying to befriend someone instead of trying to bring me down to her level. She was the only one who felt like we had levels. If people would spend more time loving each other instead of trying to tear each other down, the world would be a better place. Why do we still watch and are watched, why is there so much hate in this world. Somehow, I know I must move on with my life. I will let Barb know, I knew how cruel she is, but I think she's already aware. What was wrong with her, did she lack love in her life? Did she find pleasure in others pain, is this the reason she would try to inflict pain to others, if only she knew. The fighting between my husband and I had become more intense. I was wearing shades all the time. My eyes were all blackened and sometimes my lips were swollen. I was called into the office and told I can't come to work battered anymore. It was time for me to leave again, before he starting hurting me worse than he already had. I got another job and he didn't stop. He would show up on my job at lunch time, and sometimes he would come up to my job just to watch me work. The boss asked me to tell him not to come here anymore, and then he wanted to fight my boss. I needed to make money so I could leave him. He started acting like he was jealously in love with me, "please." That man had lost his mind. I think about the happy times we had together, and it makes me mad that we had come down to this. When we first met, I was so young and naïve. My granny told me to, "Stay, for the children, no matter what," something she lived by, but it's not working in my life. We used to travel and do so many fun things together, what happened to us? He started drinking; I heard alcohol shows your true self. He came from a dysfunctional family. I found out his dad hit his mom, and that is where he came from. His brothers and sisters witnessed their mom being kicked and beat all the time. That was something very hard to witness. My mom was mistreated too. I told myself I would never go through that, but I am them all over again. Are my sons and daughters going to be the same way? Oh, my God, I can't let this happen; I've got to get away from this. All I thought was, "My poor children, why did I stay and let this happen? I should have walked away a long time ago, but granny's words were glued in my mind. I tried to live the way she said life should be, but she was wrong. Those things only worked in her life, or did they; was she happy? Just let it ride wasn't working for me, it was time to go. I lost another job. I packed a few things and walked to my moms' house with my three babies and tears in my eyes. I'm not going back this time. My mom was glad to have us, but I knew I'd have to find work and take care of us. Where I came from the county would help you when you had children, but I didn't want handouts; I wanted a job. I started looking and found a part time job, and there were many men who worked there. One particular guy was always nice to me. I told him what I'd just gotten out of and he was in the same boat. Once again, I was living with mom. I told him I wasn't looking for anyone, but he was nice to me. He would buy me lunch and he was always there to lend an ear when my day wasn't going well. Still I wasn't going to let him near me, no, no, no. I felt like my personality was messed up right now. Once again, I had to find love for myself. I hated I let my past interrupt my optimism for the future. I was tired of being a pessimist and I became very passionate about giving my kids a good life. I started thinking about the different things I could do to give my children a better life. I changed jobs trying to run away from people. Most of them left some of the jobs I had worked at. Bus drivers often moved from driving jobs, some paid more than others. Over the years, I worked with the same folks. Before I left the job with Barb, they asked me to stay and work in the office with her. They wanted me to stay; I told them I had to go. After I left, Barb got a manager's job, which was mine. I felt running would make things better for me, but it didn't, because some of them on the new job already knew what happened to me at my previous job. They filled in the blanks telling me things, like she took my keys from my purse and came into my home while we were all sleeping, and she did things in my home. I got mad, if they knew these things were going on, why tell me now? A lot of things would have changed. She wouldn't have gotten away with so much. One driver told me these things happened before he knew and liked me. He followed them, I thought, "Thank you very much for being a part of trying to destroy my life." That really pissed me off, but what can I do about it now? There were more people who knew, and didn't like me and they still did what Barb told them to do. I was told, one day when I was asleep, one of her friends came inside my home and cut my hair. I was sleeping hard and when I woke up; I saw hair on the floor and wondered how it got there. When I went back to work she said, "Nice haircut." At that time, who would've believed me? One day I drove down the street and I saw Barb walking. I got blind with rage and ran up on the curb and hit her. She fell, I got out the car to see if she was hurt bad. She was knocked out; I pulled her into my car and was going to take her to the hospital. I felt bad, how did I allow myself to become her? I asked, "You made me do this, why did you mess with me and my life, you made me crazy; like I am now." I said, "Is it funny now?" as we got closer to the hospital, she began to talk back. I hit her hard again as I kept driving. She looked terrified as she was spitting up blood, and I knew she was afraid. I think I loosened some of her teeth. She kept talking and I hit her again. I told her to get out of my car, "You're not worth it." At the moment, I had to bring myself back to reality. She got out walking and talking. I left her there. What I did next was to cover my tracks. I went into work; I did my job and was called while on the road. They called me into the office and asked me if I did anything to Barb. I said, "No why? I knew if they believed what she said, I would go to jail. In that moment, I did her like she did me. "I said I don't know what she's talking about." I came to work on time and I repeated, "I don't know what she's talking about, you all know she doesn't like me, if I did something, why didn't she call the police?" When I saw the fear in her eyes and nobody believed her, she wouldn't call the police because it would make her look crazy; like they made me look from day one. She was shocked I got another job and walked away from that one. From that point on, every time she saw me, she got scared. She would run and go the other way. I knew those things had really messed up my mind. I needed to talk to a psychiatrist, because I felt crazy. I can't let her do this to me; I had to go on with my life; if for only one reason my children. I tried to move on, even when some people wanted to make me kill them, but I realized I didn't have to do that.

CHAPTER FIVE - IS THIS LIVING

Although I said I wouldn't go back to him, I ended up going back anyway. The children were getting older and we were trying to go on about our lives. I didn't realize my kids were being beaten by my husband. One day my manager let me go home early. When I walked inside the house, I saw my children standing against the wall; and they were crying. He had his back towards me and I heard him say to our children, "I'm going to split your necks and watch blood flow all over the floor." I yelled, "What are you doing?" My kids ran to me, his eyes were glossy and I thought, "Is he on drugs too." I told the kids to go outside, I knew he had been drinking or perhaps on drugs. He was just as mean as he could be. I got ready for the fight, and the fight was on. I said, "You're never going to hurt our kids anymore." I called the police, and they came as he was hitting me and took him away. Then the judge told him he can't put his hands on our kids anymore, or he would do serious jail time. I asked myself, "Where do I go from here." The weekend after that, he called from jail again, his new home on the weekends. I also remember one time he called, and it kind of shocked me. He was driving and he thought he was turning on a street, and instead; he hit a brick building and totaled his car. He was so drunk; he was not hurt, nor did he damage anything. I also remember one time he called, and I had to get him out of jail. He told me not to say anything to him, and he knew what he was doing. I didn't say anything because I didn't want to fight. He started having his cousins over to drink and party. They would bring food and liquor into our home. I sent my children to my moms', because they were drunk, fighting and my place was so nasty. I told my mom I was going to move away from him. Once again, we tried to stay away from him as much as we could, and we were slowly moving our thing outs. I stored our things at my mother's house. One thing about him, despite him being a drunk, he still went into work every day and he never had a hangover. Now, my children were becoming teens, and we had to have some peace in our lives, now that we were all messed up in the head, because we had so much abuse. My kids were doing well in school. They wanted to help me get away from him. They got good grades so their lives would better, and vowed never to be anything like him. I found us another place. I had a truck, and I backed it up in the driveway, and I took all our belongings out of the house, and I loaded it in the back of the truck. It felt good to leave him for good this time. According to him, everything was his except for the bed. We hurried and loaded the bed in the back of the truck, and we got out of there. My oldest son was going to be graduating soon, and I have some money saved up, I am going to make sure he is happy on his graduation day. I am so proud of him, and this is truly another milestone in his life. My children were the reason I found happiness in this miserable thing called life. Internally that is the way I felt, because of everything that has happened to me, but some positive things have happened to me as well. All my children strived to excel because they wanted to do something better with their lives other than what they have been subjected to by their father and me. They yearned to go on to a higher learning. After all the abuse, they were at the top of their classes, well-mannered and they didn't want to be like their father. I never had to go to school about their behavior; maybe they were afraid of the beating they would get from him. I taught them about love, and I told them they should strive to be successful, and not to think what they have seen between their father and I was how people lived. I wanted them to know they could have more and do better. I worked hard to make a good home for them, but I started feeling lonely. I was asked to go out by guys on my job, but I was afraid I couldn't get into a relationship; because I didn't trust any man. I hated the fact people were always watching each other. I never thought it was human nature, if no one ever looked at one another, what would this world be like? At times, I thought, "I wouldn't be able to move left or right in my life if folks didn't watch out for me, and with my luck: a good man wouldn't be coming my way." This is what I told myself for years, but maybe I was wrong. The ladies who I work with said they liked to go out to clubs, and invited me to go out with them. One night I took them up on their offer. It wasn't like I was going to pick up anyone and take him to my house; like some of them did. I was just curious and wanted to see what it was like. I decided to have some drinks with the ladies, and we had a fantastic time. Afterwards, I wanted to go again. We all went shopping for outfits to wear to the club. I found a red dress that was cute and not too revealing. We pulled up to the club. I have always felt like I was too old to go to the club, but I decided to go anyway. My granny told me clubs were the worst places, but I said to myself, "You're so wrong granny; they were having fun in there." This made me think about how much fun I had when I was in school. Guys would ask me to dance, but I had to get the hang of it first. Someone asked, "You want a drink?" I said, "Yes, gin and juice," only because my husband used to drink it. I had never been tipsy, but I was getting the hang of it. I got up and started to dance. I had the best time. The most fun I have had in a long time. While I was playing house with my hubby, there was another world out there I had yet to experience, now I know why he didn't want to stay at home with me. I started going to the club every weekend, and I would get completely inebriated. One of the guys at work asked me to meet him out at one of the clubs. I went and we really had a good time. I told him I wasn't ready for anything else, and he said, "Let's just have fun." He saw that I made it home okay and that's all I wanted for now. I was living the single life and I was having fun meeting all kinds of people, going to places I've never been before and drinking. One night I met this guy in the club named Matt. He was strong and good looking. After the club closed he wanted to take me to breakfast. Sometimes we would all go to breakfast after the club. I found myself being very attracted to Matt, and as time progressed I started to really like him a lot. For hours, we would sit and talk about everything that came to mind. If there was going to be any man who came into my life, it would be him. We would go on trips together out of town and everything was so good between us. Later I found out he has been doing this sort of thing for years. After the newness wore off, he'd be moving on. I realized this could be a sensual affair, and it's exactly what I needed. For some reason, I didn't care; I just rolled with the punches. The sex was so good with him, and every time he touched me my panties would get so wet. He would take me out and buy me expensive gifts. He wanted me to look and smell a certain kind of way. I began to wonder if I was going to be able to handle it if he was to walk away from me. I started to see a different guy, one I worked with. I didn't want to be lonely again. Matt stopped calling me and I said this was my queue to move on. I began seeing my co-worker more. I didn't want to be bed hopping all my life. I wanted to have a stable life and settle down with one man and live happily ever after, whatever that meant. I asked myself, "Who lives happily ever after?" I am always hoping and wishing everything I ever wanted and needed would come into my life, and the void in my heart would be filled with happiness. This life of mine looked like a rag torn up and blowing in the wind, what about yours? One night, Joel, (this is the co-worker I had been seeing), and I got drunk. Joel decided to have sex with me without the jimmy hat. Later after I woke up and began to take my shower, I felt like he had not used anything and I asked him why, because I could get pregnant. He didn't seem to worry about it. He said I was too old to get pregnant, and besides I was past that stage and then he laughed. Within four weeks I became sick. I felt like I had the flu, but it wasn't the flu. I told him I was pregnant and he got mad with me. He said he didn't want a baby, I said, "Well we're going to have one." He asked if he was the only one I'd been seeing, and I said "yes." I made sure I was not going to be with a lot of men at the same time. Things my mom taught me came back to my mind every once and a while. I told him he was going to be a dad. I told him, he could walk away if he wants too, but I can't. I later found out he was the boy who lived across the street from me when I was young. That little boy really hated me. I remembered I used to throw things at him and hit him on the head. I would chase him every time I'd see him. I never thought I would end up having a child from him. I really did like him, but I didn't know what I was feeling when I was young. I knew his family. Imagine, we knew the same people. At first, he was just a friend with benefits, but we have become much more than that. We now share this child. He once told me he watched me when we were young, but I thought he was saying it to get with me. It's hilarious that I know some of his family, what a small world. I told my best friend Jeana I was going to have another child. She asked, "What are you going to do?" I said, "Going to do!" I'm going to have my baby. I didn't care about what people said this baby was mine too. I can't say I am deeply in love with him, but we are both grown. We must move on with whatever life has thrown at us. I'm losing my mind, and all my other children kept wondering why I was having another child. They didn't know anything about Joel, and they knew I had left their father. My children were very interested in how this new baby was conceived. Well, all my children except for my youngest child, he was happy and looking forward to being a big brother at home. Everyone else didn't like it, but it was my life. Once Joel saw I wasn't going to get rid of the baby, he walked away from me. I didn't try to find out where he was. The ladies at work told me everything. Joel told all of management, if I called there for him to tell me he didn't work there anymore. I never tried to find out anything else about him. I went on with the pregnancy. People were so good to me; they gave me so many things for my baby. It was a blessed time for me. I was very happy until it was time to have the baby. The doctor said I needed a C-Section, I was afraid. I told mom, "You were there with my first born, and if I'm not going to make it, I want you there for this child as well. I didn't want to be knocked out; they gave me something that made me feel good. The doctor pulled my baby out and it was over. I was sick and shaking, but thank God I was still alive. That was the happiest time in my life; I wished he had been there to see her come into the world. She was so pretty. She looked like both of us, and she had his eyes, I named her Jolina. I took her home to a house full of gifts that came from friends and family. I was truly blessed. I didn't have to do much. All my friends helped me out, buying milk, clothes, and diapers. I loved all of them for all their help and support throughout this pregnancy. They said I was walking around work looking dumb, but I wasn't going to call him. I had to settle into my life and take care of my children. We didn't see or hear from Joel until my baby got sick and had to go to the hospital, and it was the first time he ever showed up. At the hospital, they asked me what happened, I told them she was breathing and acting like she couldn't get enough air. The doctor said she had asthma. Joel wouldn't say anything to me, and then he went and talked to the doctor. After they talked, we were released. I called a cab and went home. They told me to watch her because it might happen again. He never told me asthma ran his family. I wondered if she was going to have this all her life, poor baby. I was mad he was there, but I needed to find out about his family health history. I asked someone to tell him to come see his daughter; he wouldn't. Then I went over to his mother's house. Joel's mother knew exactly who I was because I used to beat up her son. She told me asthma was hereditary in their family. I knew I was going to be in for it, but it was going to be all right. James would come by to check on me and make sure I was doing all right. Then someone told me things were being said about me on the job. Barb had reared her wicked head again. I was told someone from my other job came on my current job asking about me. I wondered why Barb wouldn't leave me alone. I was curious to know if she really was a lesbian who wants to destroy someone's life, and she seemed obsessed. I felt like it was going to be a situation I had before, and I won't let it happen to me again. It was time for me to go back to work. I was determined I would not allow her and her friends mess with my home, my children or anything that is mine again. One day I was on my way to work, and I saw her walking. I needed to make it clear she wasn't going to mess with my life ever again. I went around the block and I didn't see her. I told Millie to tell her to stop messing with me or I'll tell the police what she did, or I'd have a talk with her like I did before. My friend Millie told me Barbs' two older children were going to set me up, to beat and rob me as I walked to my car. I called the police, and told them I heard some people are going to be robbed after work. The police hid, caught them, and took them to jail. Barb tried to say Millie called the police, but she told too many folks and they told me. Somehow, I had to get those folks out of my business, always wanting to mess me up. There is so much hatred in this world. Don't they have a life of their own, always digging into everyone else's business. Ever since I can remember, someone has been looking at me and being nosy. I used to say, "I must have been born under a dark star." I felt like nothing would ever go right for me, and at times I felt like I was crazy. After being told I was crazy, sometimes I believed I was. That's the type of bull that folks made me feel, if I listened to them, I would truly think I was crazy. When I came to my senses, I thought about what messed me up over the years. That's the reason I truly think there are so many insane people, some things are hard to handle. Those things may cause people to walk into a job and kill a lot of folks; when their mind can't handle being messed with. It's like everyone thinking you're the butt of the joke. Being insecure because no one ever told you that you were special, no one ever gave you hugs, or the affection you needed and prayed for. God is watching our lives play out right now. He will change some things, but you must pray you will be able to stand when he says you must stand. You must stand or you will fall, think about that and what it means. So many things seem to go wrong in some folk's lives and right into other folk lives. Barb had reared her wicked head again. My children feel like they don't belong either; did I pass it on to them without even knowing about it? Now that I am older, I look at them and wonder did it really happen. I try to help others not to feel like they don't belong. God loves us all the same; we just need to find out when we are young, so we will be well grounded. Then there are people who think they rule the world. They think they are better and higher than others, towering over them trying to make people feel like they are not worth anything. I told my children no one is better than them, so they won't feel it when they are snubbed or made to feel less than. Barb was at it again. I went into work a whole week and I didn't get a paycheck, I never missed a day of work. I went into the office and asked why I didn't get a paycheck for this week. There was a new woman working in the office who said I didn't punch in on my time card at all this week. I went into the manager's office and asked what happened. He checked and he said there wasn't a time card turned in from me this week. My manager knew I was there every day, and I insisted there had to be a mistake. He told me I had to wait until the following week to get my check. I told him I had children to take care of and I needed my check. I thought to myself why is this happening to me. I told the manager I can't wait. I asked him if he could please cut me a check from the petty cash account, and withhold all the tax deductions just like they normally have been doing with all my other paychecks. I asked if someone took my timecard out of the box, and he said yes. When I came out of his office and all I could see was everyone's eyes on me. It was that very moment I realized exactly what had happened to my time card. I walked out with a paycheck and they all just stared at my reaction. As I walked out of his office, I heard the manager say, "Barb, come into my office." When I got to my car, papers were all pulled out. Someone had ransacked my car, what were they looking for, twice in one day. I called the police and filed a report, but nothing was missing or taken that I could see. It was at this time they started taping everything that went on inside my car, but at the time I didn't know it. You see, radio tact knew how to set up the radio so it would send every conversation I was having inside my car. Radio tact was making tapes and sending them to people who knew me, still trying to destroy me. They had keys mad and would let some guy drive my car when I was on my route. My hubby told me he saw someone driving my car, when I knew I was at work. When I came back after my bus run, I started to look at the miles on my car, and it had been moved and I questioned myself how. They made those keys and went into my car. I found out they let a drug dealer at work use it, when they made sure I was out on a long route. Jim the man in the office was doing this, I was always sent out on a long route so he would have time to do whatever he needed to do. I would come back and leave and go home to get dinner ready for my kids, and thought nothing of that job. One day I drove away, when I got about a mile up the road, my tire went flat. I got someone to take it off; and it was a new tire. A man told me there was a hole in it and someone did it. He said he could put a tube inside it, that was one of those old tricks they used to do, but I let him put it in. It was time to go back to work, once again; all eyes were on me. I felt crazy at that moment, I was tripping out, and wanted to yell at the top of my voice, but I didn't. I went about my day and went home. Tears were in my eyes, why, why? All I wanted to do was live. They would not leave me alone, and then every day I was in a daze. I can't beat these people. I started letting my daughter drop me off at work on the days she was off. Things started going missing from my house; this was getting a bit overwhelming. I can't believe I couldn't find anyone to help me. I had no real proof. They made me look like I was misplacing things, but I wasn't. I wanted to kill them; I never wanted to do anything like that before. They would make me do something against the law. I bought myself a gun. I tried to talk to people, and they often told me God was watching and this was a test, well I didn't like those kinds of test. When I tried to become spiritually minded, I saw things differently. There is a part of me who wants to handle things with violence, and the other side of me who just wants to look away. I didn't do either, but those things had to stop. Someone was taping me and trying to tear me down, wanting others to hate me, but those who loved me would love me anyway. This had my life going in a different direction. If those things didn't happen to me, where would I be? Maybe they helped me to do some things I wouldn't have done. I did change some things trying to keep them out of my life. There was a driver who knocked on my door and told me he was paid to do things to my car, but that was before he knew me. I questioned, even if he didn't know me, why would he do something like that? If I would have adopted some of their philosophy, would they have liked me? My granny used to say the devil hates you when you're more evil than him, they were evil. I was not like them, and they made me grow up. I never knew I shouldn't let a man I trusted be alone with me, because he could rape me. I never knew people would hate you because you're a different color; I never knew a man could be so abusive; I never knew my children could be starved or beaten while I worked hard to take care of them. I never knew those things would mess with my mind until I die. I never knew those things would cause me to not trust anyone, ever. I've been fighting those demons all my life. I want you all to know this so you can live a better life than mine. Teach your children what they need to know, so they can defend themselves and learn who to go too. Teach them to watch what's going on, because they were being watched, even if they think they're not. I've always been told God watches all, are we all under surveillance. I never knew a lot of things. Sometimes it's not good to be in the dark about life. It will get you into trouble, because you'll be dumb founded. That's why I try to tell my children everything. Moms' husband contacted her. He told her he heard she was having a hard time. He was the father of moms' other children, not mine. He was a piece of work and made our lives miserable. I wondered if she was ready to take him back, then I thought why. But it's her life. Right away he moved in. We all thought he had a job; he left every day like he had one. I remember him being very abusive to her, always hitting her, yelling and cussing. She found out he wasn't really working and he would always come home drunk. One day she had put up a new crib, and as soon as she left, he came in and took it down and put my brother on the floor. I heard he sold it to buy himself something to drink. We wondered why she ever talked to this man; he wasn't going to do anything except bring her down. I could still remember when he was supposed to be watching the children, but he would never be home, they were left alone a lot. I can still remember when my brother was jumping from bed to bed, and he fell on the bed rail knocking a big gash in his head. If I wasn't there, he would have bled to death. That won't last long. More and more my life was a carbon copy of my moms'. I had to make some changes, at that time I planned my move. Well my hubby tried put me out of our house, it was my turn, "get out" I yelled. The only reason I was with him was because of the kids, and I felt I should give him another chance. I let him stay and he was still nasty to me. He said I was not the same girl he fell in love with, I said, "I know, I am a woman, a broken woman." He told me he wanted someone younger than me anyway. Yes, he was told some things by his older brother and he wanted someone he could control, and it's not me anymore. I didn't see him for over a year, and suddenly, he showed up at my house. He said someone told him his youngest wanted to see him, which was a lie. There was trouble in la la land. Members of my family told me the younger woman he was with, was on drugs and she was robbing him blind. I looked back at the past when I was put out of our house, and had nothing; not even a bed. Now he's in deep shit. He would come by to talk to me. He was always telling me how dirty she was doing him, but he kept going back to her. He felt I would take him back. One day there were no lights in his house. I let him stay, but as soon as he found out she was back, he walked off and I didn't see him for a while. I knew I could never trust him again. He'd come by and tell me all the things that were happening to him as he dealt with her, like I was Miss Ann Landers. She wrote for newspapers, for those of you who don't know, I read her Q & A's. He said he was taking a trip down south to visit his mom. When he got back, she moved his washer and dryer, which was something he would never buy for me. She sold them to her stepdad to get money for drugs. He would always complain to me. He didn't have too many folks to talk too, because he had burned bridges with everyone he knew. One of his relatives told me what went on. All the beatings I took from him and he would never put his hands on her. One day his aunt told me he tried to hit her, but her son hit him across his back and broke the broom while he did it. Oh, that must have hurt. From that day on, he would yell at her, but he wouldn't raise a hand to her. Her children weren't having it. One day I drove down the street and saw her. She was messed up, she couldn't walk. Every time she tried to walk, she would fall, and when she got up, she fell again. I called his aunt and told her someone needs to come get her, she said she wasn't. I went ahead and drove home; I mean why should I care? Well I did know her; I was her babysitter at one time. She came to my house and I made outfits for her. She probably went to see my husband in those very clothes. He told me he hasn't known her that long, but I heard him and his cousin laughing and talking about all of them going to see those whores. My husband and his cousin had been sneaking around for months laying up with those chicken heads. She had two little children; they had a bad life, all types of men coming in and out, plus drugs. As time went on and the kids got older, they were so ashamed of their mom. One time she was caught in a crack house. She told her friends, in front of her children, how the police told her to bend over and they put gloves up her rear end. She had no respect for them or herself. That's what he wanted, someone younger. Somehow, I felt like karma was paying him back for what he had put me through for all those years. I couldn't laugh, because I felt sorry for the children. He started coming to my house more and more. He began to become violent with me, until I threatened to call the police. He was trying to hold me accountable for all the wrong she was doing. I put him out, why would I want to hear about him or her? I became so mad, I wanted him to leave me alone, and I just wanted to move on with my life in peace. Why was he always a part of what I did? I went to the hospital; my blood pressure was 220/100, was I having a stroke? I felt my brain pulling to the left and I couldn't see out of my eyes. My brain was pulsating and nurses kept coming into my room medicating me with a lot of different pills. I could see my life slipping away. I could see lights shining into my eyes and my name being called, was I dying? My prayer was, God let me live; I need to take care of my children. I kept telling myself to wake up, wake up. When I opened my eyes, I noticed I was on a ventilator because I couldn't breathe on my own. Tears came out of my eyes and I wanted to yell, "Let me out." When they saw, me wake up, they began talking to me. The nursing staff asked me all kinds of questions, like time, date, name, and if I knew where I was at. I knew I was going to be fine, as time went by; each day I felt better. God was watching and he let me live again. The doctors said I would have some problems, but I didn't want to believe them because I felt my healing. I tried to sit up in the hospital and I couldn't. The doctor who was taking care of me wrote discharge orders for me to go home, but I would need a nurse come to my house every day. I had paralysis on my right side, so a physical therapist had to come to my house three times a week to help me with the transition of using a walker for the rest of my life, "no" I yelled. I will, with the help of the Lord beat this. I did everything the doctor told me and more. The nurse said I must have the will to be better. One day I pushed that walker out of my way; I got up and wanted to walk on my own. I took a few steps and I was happy with myself. I fell and got back up. I must get up and rebuild my life. For four months, I couldn't go upstairs. My children moved me into a house and I didn't have that crazy lady as my neighbor. I must try, after the nurse left; I got up and stepped on the first leg, but I couldn't pick up my other leg to step up. I fell towards the stairs and started to crawl up. I couldn't let those stairs defeat me. Slowly I got up on my hands and knees and taking one step at a time. That was one of the hardest things I've ever had to do in my life. The only thing that mattered to me at this point was being able to get up those stairs by myself. I counted each step as I slowly went up the stairs, after the tenth step I had to sit down for a minute and rest, and as soon as I sat down to rest my phone rang, but I couldn't answer it. I was half way up those stairs. I knew someone would show up at my house because I didn't pick up the phone. I tried harder to get to the top, I can't let those steps beat me, help me Lord. Yes, I got to the top, and then I heard they keys in the door. My daughter yelled, "Mom, mom." I proudly said, "I'm upstairs." She smiled and asked how did I get up there? I said, "I wasn't going to let those stairs defeat me, I did it, I got up here on my own." She said with tears in her eyes, "Mom you are a strong-willed lady, you just are not going to let anything beat you." I said "no." After that every day I'd pull myself up the stairs. It wasn't like I used to run up the steps, but now thank God; I can get up them every day. I felt like I could get my life back.

CHAPTER SIX- WHAT'S GOING ON

Welcome back to work, I needed to get myself some income, because checks were soon going to stop. Employers didn't care about me; they wanted to get their work done. They sent me a letter saying I needed to return to work because I had used all my sick leave. They said if I wanted to continue to work for them, I should get back to work. The doctor didn't even tell me I could go back, but they said for me to return or I would be fired. All the years I gave them and they can turn around and treat me like that. I was always there, no missing a day for many years, but I made the mistake of thinking they cared about me. My being sick meant nothing to them, only to my family and friends. I could die on that job and they would replace me before my body got cold. I had no choice but to go back to work because who was going to pay my bills? Some new folks were working there, I introduced myself to them. There was a new man that started working there and he seemed to just want to keep to himself, but he was fine. I eventually told him my name and he said his name was Andre. He just moved here and he would ask me for directions to get to different places in town. One day he asked if he could buy me lunch and I said yes. Well, he didn't know anyone, and he just wanted some companionship, and so we went to a nice restaurant. He just needed a friend, and me; not thinking, was just being friendly. I didn't understand how infatuated he became with me especially because we had only known one another for a small duration of time. I guess I really hadn't paid so much attention because I was just trying to be friendly. He started bringing me flowers and candy. I told him that was a bit much. One day his car broke down. I told him I would give him a ride home. We were like that on the job, we helped each other out. When I needed a ride, one of my co-workers would take me home because we were all friends. One girlfriend said, "You sure you want to do that?" He told others he loved me, but I didn't know that. I told her that was just hear say. He hardly knew me, we spend a lot of time together at work, and sometimes we hang out on the weekend, and yes that made us all tight. I waited until he was done working. He tried to tell me how to get to his house, I said, "Please, just tell me the name of the street." He was doing that to keep me with him, but I didn't know that at the time. He was getting me lost and it was my own home town, it was so funny. I finally pulled up to his house, he asked me to come inside and I said no. I had to get home and it wouldn't be right going inside a single mans' home. He looked at me and said, "Can't you see that I love you?" He messed me up with that. He was so young, and didn't really know what love was. Quite truthfully, I didn't know how to respond so I said, "I will see you tomorrow." As I looked up at him, he bent over and gave me a kiss which caught me off guard. I said, "I love you" and he said it again. I said, "You can't do this to me, no I'll see you at work tomorrow." I was shaking as I drove home. I didn't mean for this to happen, I was just trying to be friendly because he was new in town. What have I gotten myself into, I am old enough to be his mother so this just cannot happen When I got home I had to call my girlfriend, I said, "I trust you, please don't tell anyone." That young man said he loved me, how do I get out of this? I don't even think he knows what love is, but he thought it was real. I didn't want to hurt his feelings, but I can't let this happen, no way no how. He was a very good looking young man. I wondered why he wasn't looking at someone younger, but he said he prefers older woman. How am I going to work with him now? I tried to avoid him, and he would still find the time to come and find me wherever I was at work. I kept telling him we can't let this happen, but he'd keep trying to see me and kept saying that he loved me. My nerves were getting bad, I think maybe because I told him I was alone at home. I must have done or said something to make him think he could open and share his feelings and confess his love for me. I know what I did, I think that when I gave him more insight on my personal life, and I told him the things that has happened to me in my past he must have misinterpreted it wrong, and he thought that I was lonely looking for a man. One day he ran into the elevator with me and said, "Please let this happen, I'll be good to you, I'll take care of you, and I will give you everything that you need." He pushed the stop button; grabbed my waist and pulled me close to him so that he could kiss me. I said, "No let me go." He got mad and asked, "Why am I not good enough for you, or do you have someone else?" I said, "Baby, I'm older than you, we can't let this happen." He tried to hold on to me, I tried to push the up button, but he was pulling me and I was pushing him. He kept saying, "I love you, please, please," and tears filled his eyes. I pushed the button and ran out of the elevator and into the break room with tears in my eyes too. Everyone ran towards me and asked, "What happened, did someone hurt you and what's wrong with him?" I told them once again he said the words I love you. All my friends looked at me and yelled, "No, I told you no." I felt so embarrassed. The manager pointed to her office, I went in there first. I told her nothing had happened between us, and she said to stay away from him on the job, I said okay. She then called him into the office and told him that if he didn't stop harassing me that he would be fired from his job. I tried not to see him. After about a month, we had a meeting and we all had to be there. I saw him and he tried to talk to me and I still said no. I knew I had to act hard with him and I told him to leave me alone. I didn't have time for that mess. He wanted me and I didn't want him, he was just a kid to me; who was going to get fired over this. He tried to hold me, and I pushed back and said, "Get off me." He walked away, tears filled his eyes. I looked at him and said, "I'm sorry, I don't want you to lose your job over me." He said it again, "I love you." I just walked away crying. Vacation time was coming and I was looking forward to being away from work, it was in a few weeks. Maybe I could clear my mind and maybe he would too. My husband and I were separated, but I couldn't see myself with someone so young, even if I was alone. What did we have in common? That really hurt me, because I felt how much it hurt him. He had so much to offer to a younger woman, but not me. About a week went by and I was in a very bad car accident, and because it was a hit and run and I never saw the car that hit me. Once again, I woke up in the hospital. Many people told me what happened, but at that time I didn't remember. The doctor ordered so many kinds of tests on me, and I still couldn't remember anything. My friends and family would show me pictures, and I still didn't remember who they were. The registered nurse that was taking care of me came into my room and gave me discharge papers and she told me I was free to go home, but where was home? My family took care of me and all my friends helped too. Then one day I began to remember, and tears ran down my eyes. I wanted to know if my children were okay, and that they were with me. I was told they were fine. Many weeks passed by and I remembered more. After six weeks, I had to go back to work. I got my paperwork and went back on the road. I called in and asked where the place was, and dispatch told me a co-worker of mine told me to follow him. I did and we went back to the park at the yard. I asked him for a map, he laughed at me. I had tears in my eyes; I was born here, and didn't know my way around. Before all of this happened, I knew that job inside and out, but now I was lost. He laughed at me, and it wasn't funny. The transient ischemic attack caused to me to lose some of my memory, and he thought that was funny! I read the map over and, over again, until I found my way around. Slowly everything came back to me, or did I learn it all over again? People are so mean; all I could think about was how he laughed at me after having a stroke. The doctor told me I might have a lot of mini strokes or TIA's, and they may cause me to lose some of my memory. Somehow, I had to hide this. I started writing down things, because I might need the notes. Daily I looked at them to help me along throughout the day. Then my memory started to come back. We all went to lunch like we used too, I became very quiet. I didn't feel comfortable talking to people the way that I used too because everyone would tell me how my personality had changed. They told me that I was not the same, but I didn't remember how I was before, what could I do about that? I listened to what the pastor said about life. I thanked God for life and how he kept me around to write this book. As he said, everyone has their own story, and some of us can't get away from ourselves. People always have an opinion about what you should do, but they're not you and they don't know how much a person can tolerate. People always talk about what they would do in a situation, but in actual reality we all have different ways of reacting to certain things. Some of us tend to try to hide our feelings, while other folks are in everyone else's business and they spread gossip about things that they do not know anything about. I know they watch and talk about you, because you don't do what they do, they act a certain way. They should try to love you and move on, but people are always out to hurt one another. I walked past folks and they start to talk about me, they don't know what they are talking about. If they would try talking to me, they would know the truth about me, but that's too much for them to do. They love to think bad about everyone, as though they haven't done anything wrong or distasteful. Pain has followed me all my life and I can't shake it; it's a deep pain. Maybe my life would have been different if I hadn't met those people. Life would have been very peaceful if I had just turned left instead of right. I would be living lavishly. I picture opening my eyes and I'm in Hawaii, with warm breezes blowing into my face as I try to fall asleep. We spent the day swimming and playing on the beach, drinking cold drinks, and just having fun. Doing everything that made me happy, and this was just a vacation, I planned to see the world and everything I would like to see. I would go shopping and buy everything I wanted, let me get that hat for the sunshine. It's so beautiful here, tomorrow we're going to go jet skiing. After that, we are going to South Africa then to Peru to climb the hills and sample all the food, maybe for a week. The world is so beautiful and I plan to see the whole world, and buy any and everything that made me happy. Things I only dream about. As I daydreamed I got a call from Jeana's husband, she had been taken to the hospital. It was her heart. I rushed to see her. We were like sisters; that's how close we were. Tears filled my eyes; I said to myself, "Will I lose the only best friend that I have ever had?" We went to grade school, and grew alongside one another. I was there when she said she was getting married, and she was there when I got married. We were there for each other when we had our children. Only God knows what's going to happen when I walk into that room. It didn't look good; they said her heart was enlarged. I couldn't stay there too long; it hurt me to see her like that. When I got back home, I started thinking about all the good times we had as little girls and in high school. She was my sister. She progressed all throughout the week and she was getting stronger every day. The doctor released her to go home after one week, and the doctor told her that she had to change her lifestyle. She called me crying because she found out that her husband had been cheating on her while she was sick and in the hospital. I called her from work and told her I would stop by her house after I got off work. The doctor released her to go back to work after about six weeks, and he told her that she still needed to take it easy at work. We would call each other on our breaks. She was promoted and so she had a better job, however the other ladies didn't seem to like her. As soon as she took the position, they stopped doing their work, so she had to work more hours at work, and she didn't get any overtime for the time that she stayed over because it was considered straight time. She was trying so hard to please people. What she didn't know was that the lady her husband was cheating on her with turned out to be a co-worker who looked in her face every day and act as if she had done nothing wrong. My friend would cry every day, and I told her she could only take so much emotional pain, and on top of everything else her husband was cheating on her too. One day she called me because she didn't get my RSVP for her daughters' baby shower on Friday. I said, "Are you kidding, you know I'm coming," she said, "I'll call you when I get home." When I got home she called me and said, "We got to go for a ride." She came and picked me up and she drove me all the way on the other side of town. She pulled up to this house, I suspected it was the woman her husband was cheating on her with, but I didn't see her hubby's car; she did. She said, "Let's get out," and we walked up to the house. She banged on the door, at first no one answered; she kept banging on the door. Her hubby answered the door and asked, "What are you doing here?" She said, "I found paperwork that you're buying this house and your girlfriend is living here." That lady came out the door and said, "That's right." Jeana went crazy; she pushed her way into the house. All I could hear was glass breaking, screaming, and yelling she was tearing that lady up. Her husband was trying to pull her off, and when he finally got her off the lady; he pushed her to the door. He said, "I'm coming home and I'll talk to you there, please go home." I walked her to the car and she was a mess, so I drove. She started having chest pains; I immediately took her to the emergency room. I called her husband and told him where we were. He came shortly after I called him and I felt like she was in good hands. Although, I still couldn't look at him, but I told him goodnight, and then I gave her a kiss on the cheek and I drove myself home. I'm the one who got them together; I thought he would be good to her and in ways he was. The way he cheated on her while she was sick and in the hospital cut deep, almost as if he had cheated on me. She was my sister, that's what I called her. He made her so mad, he didn't think about her condition. He should have hidden those papers. When I walked into my house, my son told me that Jeana, my best friend had died, all I could yell was, "no, no, no." My heart went out to her children. Her daughter was about to have her first baby, and she died before seeing him. She knew it was a boy. She told me, "I'm going to have my first grandson; she always wanted a boy and couldn't have any more children. My life would never be the same without her. I had other friends, but not like her. I closed my eyes and saw us running to the store to buy candy, jumping rope, singing, talking about boys, making plans for our lives, hiding from our siblings; we were very much like sisters. I still feel the pain, when does it go away? My husband came around, he was good company for a while, but he began to try to take over; I knew it was time for him to go. I won't let him piss me off this time. I can't let him make my life a living hell again, he had to go. Sometimes you must get rid of all the toxicity, and negative energy in your life. I had to move on, no more fighting, no more being hit, no more black eyes or fat lips, it was time for him to exit. I called my mom to see if she was all right, and she was. I thought about how she went through all that abuse until her husband died, and a little of her soul died right along with him. We should never let ourselves feel like we can't live without another human being because we can. Not everyone is cut out to be someone's mate. That's what we were told when we were younger, and we tried too hard to find that type of life. Some of us will never be moms, dads, or someone's mate. People shouldn't be made to feel bad because they don't fit into that mold. These are the kinds of things that could leave a person's mind warped, if you're not like this or that; will they love you or will they hate you for trying to be you. I was told I had a chronic illness, and this book must come to life before I leave this world. Like I said before, we are always being watched, as you read the pages of this book, I know you must wonder. Have you ever talked to someone, and then hours later you find out the person who you were just talking with was dead? Well, this is what happened to my brother. I was my mom's first child and then she had others. He was mom's first son. We were very close and my mother would always tell me to make sure my brother was all right because she worked all the time. I was the one who was always responsible for taking care of my brothers and sisters. My other siblings were the opposite from me, and they would always tear up and break things in the house, but my brother would always help me out any way he could. I loved my brother. When you are young, people tend to watch you to see what you're going to do and what you're going to have. He started out on the wrong side. Mom would get calls about him, and the police officers would always tell her that they were going to take him away from her, and that would hurt her to the core every time the officers would tell her that. One night, just before daylight, I was awakened by men yelling and our door was kicked in, the kids were crying. I thought it was a dream until the police came into my bedroom and told me to get out of my bed. They were looking for guns, I said, "There are no guns in my room." I didn't know there was one, they tipped me off the bed and flipped the mattress over and they found the gun my brother hid under my bed. I couldn't believe he did that. I knew he loved me and meant no harm. He felt it was a safe place and no one would look there. The police took my brother and the gun away, and we didn't see him for four years. My mom would visit him, but we couldn't. After his time was up, he came home and said he would never get into trouble again. He said he was going to marry his girlfriend. His life went on; the police always messed with him until he got older, now he is dead. I still love him, he had some bumps and bruises in life, but he will be missed. He's in a better place; all the suffering he had is gone and he's in the arms of God now. I know God watches all and he knows why things happen, we will understand one day when he lets us know. All I've been through seems so little when I see how bad it can get and may be getting worse. I had to take my van to the shop, and the mechanic told me he found the problem. He said there were some wires that were mixed up, and then he told me how he could fix it. He said someone grounded the speakers to one of the lights, something was rigged. I felt it was the same listening device that was put into my other car, but no one would believe me. He asked me if the radio worked, and I said yes. He was not an expert on radio installation, so he wouldn't know anything about it. Someone told me I used to work with, and they used to rig up the managers' cars, so they could call us from their cars. Apparently, this was done to my van; I got the van out of the shop and parked it. If they heard what we were saying again, they were messing with my life again, when will this ever end? My family and I have been through so much, and it may never stop. Something began to happen to me and I became sick, the Doctors didn't know what was wrong. I was the only one who got sick in the house. I wondered what happened to me, did someone put something in my food, why don't they know what's wrong? I was going to the hospital weekly. I couldn't breathe; I've never had this happen to me. I know it sounds crazy, but when something was done to me, I knew what was going on with me. One doctor said I had COPD, another said asthma, and then another doctor said it was a heart condition. They didn't know what was wrong with me, and that hurt me; what was I supposed to do? I was taking so much medicine, until I was out of it all the time. I slept for days and hours. Then one morning I didn't take all the pills, I stayed awake and the next day I got a little better. The fewer pills I took, the better I felt. I wondered why my doctor prescribed all that medication to me because it didn't make me feel better, all that medication would make me feel worse. I thought to myself is someone trying to kill me. This had to stop, I must find out who was doing this. Barb was gone, I heard she had died and it wasn't a pretty sight. I heard she had cancer and they say she suffered badly. I think this was what she got for all the nasty things she did to so many people. I didn't feel anything for her, it was like I couldn't feel, because of all the pain she put me through when she was trying to destroy my life, and she would always laugh about the things she did to me, she thought it was funny. Millie told me she cried for her children to help her, but they wouldn't. You see, when children are taught to live any kind of way, and do anything they want too, they just live like they were taught. If she didn't show them love and let them do any and everything, that's how they grew and lived. If she taught them to hate, that's all they knew. That's why it is so important to teach our children how to love, without love in this world; there would be so much turmoil, evil and wickedness. I have found forgiveness in my heart for everything that has happened to my family and I, but that doesn't take away what happened. I don't trust people, and it's hard for me to make plans to go anywhere or do a lot of things. I really don't want people in my business; it kind of makes me have crazy thoughts. Many people think I am eccentric. At times, I can't get away from who I am. I've been known to say a lot of crazy things. Like one day I walked into the office and asked a lady what was going on, you guys need to hire more men. I heard I had sex with forty men on this job. I told the lady you must hire more men, so I can do what everyone says I do. I yelled, "Forty men don't even work here," as she laughed with me. They quickly stopped telling that lie. The lady said, "You're laughing about it!" I said yes, because it's not true. Actually, not everything bad has happened to me was on the job. The co-workers I hung out with were truly my friends. They helped me through a lot of different things I was going through when I was down, and they tried to help me even if the situation got crazy. I loved to sing, and the haters did talk about me. Some of my friends started booking me gigs to sing at some clubs, and when I would sing at the clubs it would take my mind off all the bad things in my life. I wrote this on a napkin to a man one day: If you say you want to be my man, there's something that you don't understand, I ain't got no time to play any games, and my name isn't Susan it's Elaine. They said I was trying to be smart, but it was just my heart, because of all the wrong things, it made me want to lash out. Some said because my step-father molested me, maybe I acted out; even after I had grown up. Deep down inside, maybe I wasn't over what happened to me. All the wrongs that were done to me had somehow caused me to just live anyway and anyhow. I started drinking and not caring what happened to me. It was just too much to handle, way too much. Sometimes women like me live their lives being promiscuous. I have always remembered what my mother told me, and I try not to live my life regretting all the wrong things I did. They will come back and bite you, so I stopped myself from doing somethings. Children will hear and see what's going on too, and it could cause a lot of embarrassment. They will try not to make the same mistakes you made, but your mistakes will follow them. They call it a legacy; sometimes it could cause the rise or fall of your realities. As I started getting older, I looked at life a little differently, and I thought about all the things that happened to my family. I thought about the day a truck hit my bus. I was driving down the road with Carmen and the children, and a green truck came speeding heading towards us. I could see him coming fast, weaving in and out around cars. I stopped and I said to her, he might hit us, which is why I stopped moving. I thought he hit a car, that's when I got scared. I said, "Girl, he's going to hit us," and before I could get it out, he hit us very hard. The mirror on the truck popped my mirror off. My window was opened and the mirror flew into the window and hit me on the head, I blacked out for a minute. I could hear Carmen yelling my name. I opened my eyes and wondered where I was, and who she was yelling at, telling them they hit us. Carmen and Supervisors said I told them I needed an ambulance. Instead, they sent the nearest bus driver to come help me out. However, I thought they were only trying to cover up they're at fault accident. Then I remembered the other bus driver told me to follow him to the base. Somehow, I remembered how to drive the bus and I followed him back to the base. Then someone drove the bus away after we went into the gate. A man walked me into the office and they began to ask me things and I could talk. I remembered telling them I needed to go to the hospital. They said I looked fine. I kept telling them my head was hurting. That was a job that didn't back me, I have done nothing wrong, but they knew all the dirty things they helped people do to me. I went to the hallway and called my son and told him what happened and to come get me. The next thing I knew I was in the hospital with tubes and things coming out of me. The doctor asked what happened to me, and I told him what I knew and a truck hit my bus. The doctors told me I had a stroke and my supervisor said the truck supposedly hit my vehicle never happened, and that I was crazy; nothing happened on the job. I called some of my co-workers and Rosa. My co-workers and Rosa told the nursing staff at the hospital the same story I just finished telling the doctor, and I said, "the lady who told you I was crazy is a liar." My son called the police department, and he went and got my car from their lot, where they said I didn't work. She should have been fired, but she was the bosses' girlfriend. After four days, they let me go home, the job began calling me and telling me to come back to work. Mind you, I had a stroke. They wanted a woman who just had a stroke to come back to work and drive on the road with other people like it was all right. That's just wrong, they covered the accident up, they took the bus to the shop and fixed it up, but as I left, I put the mirror that hit me on the head in my purse. I showed it to the nursing staff. I had to turn the ringer off my phone, the girl at the office kept calling me, how was I supposed to get well? The doctor told me to rest, and I was going too. Then they didn't want to send my paycheck, and I called a lawyer. Miss Office lady was also my landlord. She came by to get the rent, how was I to pay rent when she didn't send my paychecks? The lawyer called and said they had to give me my checks, but when; was the question? After two months, she had the heat turned off in my apartment, my children and I needed heat. I called a friend and she helped me move my things out. I put my furniture in three different places. My children and I went to stay at my mother's house. She still wouldn't leave me alone; she called my moms' house until mom told her she would call the police. My husband was giving me a little child support, and the money was used to feed my children. Meanwhile, I was looking for work. When I was released from the hospital, the doctor said I would be able to go back to work, but he told me, I shouldn't go back there; too much stress. I called a friend who took over a new job. He said when the doctor clears me to go back to work; I could work for him, thank God. After a month, I was ready to go back to work. I talked to the lawyer to see if I could get the money that was owed to me. He said they must pay me. A check came, but it wasn't what they owed me, but on paper, it looked like they cheated once again. I took what it was and then Miss Office lady wanted her rent. Well I moved upstairs in the house mom lived in. I didn't have it all, but I did pay some money to her. She was the one who caused me to get behind. I lost my apartment, and my car was repossessed, but I didn't lose my mind although that's what the rumor was in the streets. After I went to work for the other guy, my landlord took me to court and garnished my check for the rent I owed her. That didn't break me either. After it was paid, I got something from her dad who tried to take me to court for a floor. That was a lie, the lawyer went by to see if a new floor was put down, and it wasn't, so he wouldn't be touching my check. Life went on, I wasn't left alone, but I became happy. Life was good again my entire house was back together. My children were happy and that's all I needed. Then Miss office lady started sending Mr. Joe to spy on me. At first I felt he might be a friend, but he told things about me. When Millie called me, I knew he was up to no good. I told him not to come back over to my place. Again, life went on and I tried to forget about the whole thing, but can I forget? Sometimes I wondered about what my purpose was supposed to be, and what I was supposed to be doing with my life. I couldn't see it yet. Just when I thought I knew things would change, my sister and I made amends, because we knew how short life was.

CHAPTER SEVEN-THESE ARE MY FRIENDS

Jeana was the girl next door, as soon as we moved in; she came over to play with me. We shared dolls and other toys, but there was something I didn't know until later in our lives. Our city was changing the bus routes. We had to walk to school each day; there and back. All the kids in the neighborhood met at one corner, and we all started to walk to the high school. It turned out to be twenty-one kids. When we all got to the top of the hill on the heights, we took a final lap to school. Sometimes it was snowing; we all tried to make it. Jeana was the so-called boss, she was a leader. We all followed her; she always told us we would need to be educated for our future. She was the one I told all my secrets too, but when she started telling me things, I broke down and cried. Then I felt she had been through some bad things too, just like me. One night after my mother went to sleep, I heard her throwing rocks at my window, and she said "Let me in." I went down and let her in. She said "Hide me." I wanted to know what was going on. She said, "When the police come, tell them you don't know where I am, please." I told her to go into my bedroom. My mom was asleep when I let her in, the police banged on the door and they woke my mom up. She called me out of my bedroom and asked if I had seen Jeana, I said not since school and I asked her why. She said Jeana was missing and if I see her to give the police department a call and I said okay. After they were gone, mom knew I was lying and asked me, "Where is she?" I told her she was in my bedroom; I said she had been abused. Then I

104

said, "Mom please let her stay here until the morning, so she could call her dad." She told me for years her step-father had been having sex with her on a regular basis and she wanted it to stop. She was scared to tell her mom and she kept that inside for years. We were teens and he had sex with her for seven years; she was sixteen. I knew when boys came around; her step father acted like she was his. At that time, I thought he was just trying to be that father that she never had, but he turned out to be more sinister. Boy, we cried so much that night, until we fell asleep. Mom called me the next morning to get up for school. Mom told Jeana she would have to work it out with her family and to call her mom. Jeana picked out something from my closet to wear. We started to walk to school, as we walked, I told her to tell someone at school, but in those days, things like that fell on deaf ears. She was going to talk to her mom when she got home. When it was time to walk home, Jeana had left early. For the next few days I wasn't allowed to see nor talk to her, why did her mom want to sweep this under the rug? When I finally saw her, she was angry about how her mom was handling it. She wanted her mom to put him out, but she didn't because she had children from him still in their home. I saw my best friend turn into a monster. She was full of hatred for him. She told him if he ever touched her again, she would kill him. Mom told me to back away I had too, but I felt she needed a friend. We were best friends and I couldn't tell mom the things me and her shared. I had to talk to Jeana about school. I told her she was a good student and she couldn't let this mess her up bad. We were almost out of school, I told her, "You will mess up if you let this consume you; you must find a way around it." All those years of anger she held inside, as weeks went on, she said to herself, "I will not let this consume me." I tried to plan little things to make her forget about it, she was going to run away. He stayed at their house, and she was instructed to say nothing to her mother or step-father, and she was told not to speak about what her step-father was doing to her. One day he started getting loud with her and he hit her. Then they began to hit each other, her anger was giving her strength, she was yelling, "You took my innocence, you messed up my mind, I hate you." As she was hitting him, her mom was yelling and crying. They were hitting each other hard. I had to call the police; she was trying to kill him. She hit him with a stick, I yelled for her to stop. The police finally came and pulled them apart and handcuffed them both. When she told, them he molested her, they took her hand cuffs off and he went to jail. I didn't understand why her mom was mad at her. She hung her head and had the saddest look I had ever seen. Jeana had been saving her money from an after-school job. The next day she moved out of her moms' house. She sent me a note when graduation came, I didn't get a chance to go to it. Months went by and she finally came around to visit me. She told me she had a better job and invited me to her new apartment. It seemed like life did go on for her, or did it? No one knows just what it does to a person when they are raped or abused, but to that person, they feel it. You see it, sometimes they hide it, but it's always there. Sometimes I walked inside myself and I had everyone who did something wrong to me inside one maze, a very big maze. They were trying to find their way out, and I tricked them; by promising them their hearts desire. This place only caused pain, but they didn't know it yet. They were told by a speaker which way to turn, but they were going deeper and deeper into the maze. It was cold and wet, yet they followed the voice. A few of them thought to themselves, they were getting deeper and stopped following the voice. Some turned right when they were told to turn left. As they were trying to get out of the maze of their ways, they failed; because there were holes they fell into, twisted their ankles. They did it to themselves, because they didn't follow the voice. I could hurt them, but what good would it be to me to be so evil. Then the dream ends, and I'm still in the same boat they put me in. Why couldn't I be like them? As time went by, they did more things to hurt themselves, and I didn't have to lift a finger; you reap what you sow. Everything was not always bad, like when I told you about some good things before Jeana died. I had to tell her I was going out with her cousin, who was a bit younger than me. Like I said before, my friends and I from work started going out every weekend. Some folks said when you bar hop; you're looking to get laid, not me. I had no life and it was just a joy to be away from all the mess in my life. Every weekend I went there, I was being watched by her cousin, he wouldn't leave me alone. I kept telling him to get lost, but he would say things like, "I want to get lost inside of you." That kind of pick up line showed how young he was. I asked, you're not even twenty-one, are you?" and he said, "Yes I am." But I knew he had to be young, he was very nice; even when I brushed him off, and he remained nice. So, I started speaking to him and one night he asked me to dance. He had studied me and done his homework; he knew I loved to dance. He was putting moves on me, and I just couldn't let him out dance me. That was something I've always hated, for a man to out dance me. After the night was over, he was still a gentleman and said, "See you next week." Then he got smart and said, "I out danced you tonight." He had a way about him that made me laugh, he said, "Work on those dance moves, you were kind of rusty." That pissed me off, but we both laughed it off, but it wasn't funny to me. The next week he was there and ready to dance, we danced all night long. When it was time to go home, he asked me if I would meet him for lunch later. He knew where I worked and lived. I thought folks always watch me no matter what I did. I said, "Yes call me." He said, "No you call me, and say seventeen and hang up and I'll call you back. I asked, "Damn, am I one of seventeen women"? He said he was a business man and only answers what he wants; he also said everything has its own time. He was a very a bright young man. Friends told me about him and how well he was doing for himself, especially being so young. He told me where to meet him for lunch. The place was nice, I felt out of place, because I worked in jeans, but when he saw me he called me over to the table. We had a good lunch, when I had to go back to work; I thought to myself, "Umm he's nice and knows how to treat a woman, if he keeps this up, I may just fall in love." Then I thought, "You know all he wants is to get me into bed, but he is doing a damn good job." It would turn out to be more and we never talked about sex, that's what I liked about him, he was taking his time to know me. We went to the movies and found places we could dance too; this went on for about four months. He knew I loved to dance. Then one day he said his birthday was tomorrow, and he wanted to do something special. I knew it was time, without him saying, he wanted sex now; and I was ready too. After the club, he rented a room and he asked me to spend the night with him. I said yes because I knew it was time. We had soft romantic music playing, a bubble bath and chilled wine. My baby put it on me, so soft and smooth. Then we went to sleep and the morning came. I was glad it was the weekend, because I would have called out, had it been a work day. It was time to go, business was calling him. All I could say was, "Umm, what a night, I think I'm in love." We went everywhere together; this love was growing inside both of us. He told me, "You treat me like I always wanted to be treated, and I love you." He told me things about himself and this was the happiest time in his life. Everything was going strong, until his so-called baby's mama came around. She was always asking for money. I didn't say anything about his life, because he was like that when I met him. He loved his little boy, I'm not knocking that, but she tried to push me and she didn't know how. I would look at her when she came to his place cursing and yelling, he would give her money and she would leave, so I held my peace. I knew he loved me, he told me a lot about his childhood. Turned out I knew his mom, when she found out we were a couple, she hit the ceiling. She told him I was too old for him, that's when all the stuff hit the fan. I told him, "I'm not going to come between you and your mother, I love you, but I have to walk away if there's going to be a conflict." Everyone was trying to tear us apart, and then I started staying away from his place. People were calling me names and telling him to use me because I was a few years older than him. They told him just how dirty he should treat me. I wonder if they thought I was going to take that. So, with a broken heart I walked away. I moved and changed my phone number, if he was going to listen to everyone but not his heart, I'm gone. I found out the first little boy turned out not to be his, and it just broke his heart; the girl's granny told him the kid was not his. One day about five months from the last time I saw him, he found out where I lived and showed up at my door. He had tears in his eyes telling me how he made a mistake, but he still loved me and couldn't get me out of his mind. By that time, he was married to a young girl, his mom found her for him. He didn't care if I felt hurt and I couldn't make it without him, but now here he is. Why should I even talk to him? Everything seemed so good at first in his little world, but then it just fell apart. I found out his mom set him up, she told him the young girl was close to his age and she could give him lots of babies. She knew he wanted children and I couldn't have anymore; but they forgot about love. I kissed him softly on his cheek and told him he must go home and work it out. I can't mess around in no one's marriage. Tears filled his eyes as he turned and walked away. I wanted to tell him please stay, but he made this love fall apart. Somehow, I knew that would not be the last time I'd see him. He got my new phone number and address from someone, but I didn't know from who. One day he called and wanted to talk. I talked with him; he started by telling me how unhappy he was. He told me his mom set him up with that young lady. She was a virgin, and he said every man wants to be a virgin's first. I didn't believe him, he wanted her or it wouldn't have gotten to that point. Then things started happening on my job. Some of the employees from my old job came over to work at my new job. I knew that meant trouble. In a week, they had things happening; sitting around talking about me and starting rumors. They would laugh when I walked by, acting like kids, but I wasn't having it. They were the same people who started the rumor about the forty men I was supposed to have had sex with, I laughed that rumor off. But this is a new day, I can't let that happen, my heart was broken from losing the love of life and I was feeling kind of bitter. Just as I was about to blow up; one of my friends stepped in and pulled me away from my mind. I was going to get my gun and end it all, but that would have been my end. She told me they were not worth losing another job or my life. It took a very good person to walk away from them that day, but I did. Daily I stayed away from them, but the rumors kept going on about me. One day I was called into the office about lies on me again. I had to go for drug testing, I didn't mind because I was taking pills for high blood pressure and my Doctor faxed over that information. I went and had the test and the results came back clean, like I knew it would. These are the things that have been going on for quite some time, all the lies and I was sick of it. I asked to talk to the manager. I told him the things they put me through on my last job. When I lost my last job, they tried to break me down, but that was not going to happen. They started doing the same things, calling my house, and hanging up the phone, messing with my car and flatten my tires. They made me want to load up a gun and shoot them, but that would only hurt me. I didn't want to get myself in trouble over that, but it must stop. So, I got some cameras and put them all around the house. Someone told them I had cameras all around my house and they stopped coming there. Who can I go to, and who is going to help me? I knew other people knew about what had been going on, but no one would come forward, now who can they be afraid of? Barb can't still be doing this, I felt like it was one of her old friends, another hater, one that hasn't reared their head, but I will find out; if it's the last thing I do. I got called into the office again over some he says she say shit. I didn't want to say anything, but I did. I said, "I don't do anything against the law, on the job or off and these were just lies." I had it, I really didn't care if they believed me or not. I worked for them for a while, and why now; suddenly, why would I turn bad like that. I was the employee of the year and again employee of the month, I asked why would I do just the opposite? Mrs. McGee knew me from my other jobs and spoke up for me; she told the office personnel that those things happened at the other job. She said my bus had just passed as the cleanest on the lot. I went to lunch, and when I came back, someone had emptied and poured two or three garbage cans full of trash from the front of the bus to the back, and it stank. The manager had to make the ones he felt put it on there; clean it off. He asked if I knew which one did it, I didn't know and I wasn't going to point fingers, because I could've been wrong. There are so many haters in this world. They get mad if you have more than they do, or want what you have. Some folks don't know it's all material and in the end when we all die, you can't take it with you. Some say they don't care, they still can't bear to see other have things, and that's why they try to take it away; that's sad. As soon as I got home my phone rang, it was a co-worker named Rosa. She asked me about what happened at work and I told her. She said she needed to talk to me, I said for her to come over. She told me her boyfriend put her out and she began to cry and told me what was going on. He was a no-good dead beat father, he didn't work and she paid all the bills. I asked, "He put you out, out of a place you pay for and it's in your name?" He took her money weekly, paid the rent and utilities, but any money left; he kept. He always spent her money, the way he wanted, he dressed in the best clothes and she came to work raggedy. She told me of the beatings he gave her and the verbal abuse. She asked if she could stay the weekend, so I let her stay. Monday, she was going to the bank, he didn't know she had a little money, she got from her mom. She said she was looking for a place, by the end of the week, she should have a place, and she did. He started calling the job looking for her, he even tried to come into the job, but the guards wouldn't let him in. He was so mad with her; he trashed her car, tore it up so bad, it wouldn't run. I gave her rides to work; he didn't know how she was getting around. She rented a truck, took the things her mom gave her and moved into her new place. He knew we were friends, but he didn't know where I lived. At first I thought she would be weak, like I was and take him back, but she was stronger than I was. Then she wanted to go to the club with the rest of us. None of us had a man, just kids. All our children were taken care of when we went out. We had my babysitter keep them and she was getting paid well. So off we went bar hopping. Rosa was a drunk and often one of us had to stop her from leaving the bar with any Tom, Dick, or Harry. Horny and whoring, that's all she thought about, I think she wanted to destroy herself because her relationship didn't work. Sometimes after the club, we would go get some food and the party was on until the next morning. Everyone from the club went to the same eatery. As we were all eating, Rosa started crying, and it turned into screaming. Everyone in the place wondered what was wrong with her. The manager came over and said she would have to go. We had to pay for our food and we wanted to eat our food. She wouldn't stop; I pulled her out of the place and told someone to get my food. I kept asking her what was wrong. She fell to the ground, I said, "I can't pick you up, you're bigger than me, get up and tell me what's going on." She missed that dead-beat man. She didn't want to be alone, and she had been lying down with everyone and she still felt lonely. She still had us as friends. Then I said, "You're just drunk and you don't have to be alone, damn it; get into the car." Everyone else came out; as we drove home we all ate in the car. We made it to her house and I asked her if she was going to be okay, she said yes. I said, "You know you need to lay off some of that drinking, because you are begging." I told her I was going to call her when I got home; she took her food and went inside her house. I called her as soon as I got home. We talked until 7:00 in the morning. We didn't have to go to work, but it was time for me to go to bed. I hung up after I knew she wasn't going to do any harm to herself and she was sober. Rosa called me about 8:00 that night and said, "Let's go out around 10:00 p.m. I told her I really didn't want to go, and she said she would go by herself. Rosa called me at 3:00 a.m.; I asked her what was going on. She said the police had just left her house, and I asked her why. She told me she was loud at the bar and she flirted with the officer. He told her he would handcuff her if she didn't calm down. She told him he better do her right, I said, "No you didn't, and he took you to jail." She said no and she took him to bed. She said he was a married man. He parked his police car at her house, came in and got some and then left. I thought they were there to serve and protect, but this was his service. Rosa was such a whore; they did it without protection, knowing he was married. The next day she said her nosy neighbor, who watched everything that went on; she was sick of it, asked her why the police officer was at her house. She counted everyone who went into her house, and just wanted to know someone else's business. I went to Rosa's house to sit and talk for a while, and her neighbor came over being nosy once again. I didn't like her, but Rosa didn't let it get under her skin. She wanted to know why the police was at Rosa's house. I told Rosa not to tell her, but she kept asking, but she wouldn't tell her why the officer was there. That woman was the nosiest. Sometimes when I went to Rosa's house, I would go to the bathroom; I could hear her walking in the room above the bathroom, like she was watching folks go to the bathroom. Maybe she had cameras looking down into the bathroom. One day Rosa wasn't home and I waited for her on the porch. The nosy neighbor asked me to come inside her place. I went up there, when I got inside I saw monitors all around the house, and I asked her why. She said it was for security. I asked, "Who needs that much security?" it was a very good neighborhood. One room she didn't let me see, I believe she was watching Rosa from her house. When Rosa got home I said, "Girl that woman is watching your every move, I just want you to know. We started looking for cameras. One night me and Rosa went to the store and left her nieces in the house by themselves, they were all teens. While we were shopping, she got a call that the police were at her house. We rushed back and found out a complaint came from that witch upstairs. She said the kids were making too much noise, but she would do nasty things to get on people nerves. She started going into the basement to mess with Rosa's washer and said she said Rosa was stealing her light bulbs. I told Rosa the woman was bipolar. She would mess with everyone she could when they came to visit Rosa's. She has lived in the house for fourteen years. We thought her and the landlord were going out with each other. One day Rosa had a party and she told her to come down. She showed out laughing and talking crazy, we tried to be good to her, because we knew she didn't have it all. She knocked on Rosa's door one day and said Rosa was stealing her mail and she wanted it back. Rosa tried to tell her she didn't have it. When she went back upstairs, she called the police, they quickly knew who she was, and she had been doing this for many years. The witch lady was on the war path. She told the whole neighborhood she paid Rosa's rent and they were going out together. I couldn't put my finger on it, but I knew that was so wrong, but the police officers couldn't do anything about her, and she would get away with it. The witch lady started marching up and down the street with a sign, which read every bad thing she could say about poor Rosa, and she came home from work to see the sign. Everyone told Rosa she should move, she said she couldn't afford to move. That sick woman said Rosa stole her motorcycle, she could barely drive her car;

most of the time she was drunk, how could she ride a motorcycle? Her meds were not working because she drank. I said, "What, how much more could you take, she could hardly stand, how was she going to ride a bike that big?" Witch lady was a crazy old woman; she needed someone to help her. One day Rosa came home and the fire department was there. That lady had started a fire in the garbage can. She said she burned Rosa's mail because it was no good. Again, the police were called, but this time they said they had to do something. That time they called her family; they went over and had her put in the mental hospital. They took her as she yelled, shouted and cussed all the way. She said Rosa was trying to take what she had, but she had nothing. She was sicker than I thought. Why do they let crazy folks on the streets? What could have made that lady so crazy, bugging for no reason at all? Rosa new after her stay in the hospital she would be coming back to bug her again. Poor Rosa, she said she was going to move before she killed everyone in that house. She began looking for a new place to live. Rosa went into the basement to wash clothes and her washer was full of toilet paper. That witch did it; everything Rosa had in the basement has been torn up. She was so upset, she worked so hard to get everything she had, but she can get more. That's not a reason to let her mess over her. Rosa told me she was leaving town. She got her money together and began loading her truck. I'm going to miss her, but we will stay in touch. She's going back to her home town in the sought; I hope she made the right move.

Charles Lee Robinson Jr. & Elaine Denise Robinson

CHAPTER EIGHT – LIFE GOES ON

Life goes on. I started feeling sick again and it was time to go back to the hospital. They said this could just take me out, but I put it in God hands. That's what I kept saying, but I didn't get to know right away. They said water was building up around my heart. "Why, why, why won't they tell me or do they know how to stop it." I kept saying, "I'm too young for this." I tried hard not to panic, but sometimes I just wanted to yell and scream. Most of the time I couldn't sleep, I shook as I cried out. So, I wrote these things to you and maybe you can make sense out of it. I walked and talked to myself. What do you do when doctors can't do anything for you? Every day I said things to my children, so if I don't wake up one day, they can make it without me, because I'm so close to them. They're all I got other than God. They had become my world. When I would go through things, those kids kept me; in bad times, just looking at them made me want to try harder. People put their foot in my life, but my children made it worth it. Their smiles made me happy, but in all, God was the one who knew all those things that happened. Right now, is the opening of my heart. Some people wouldn't have made it through all the things I did. Some would have taken their own lives. I think they thought they had me to that point, but they didn't, because no one knew what I felt. Sometimes I take a good look inside of myself, and everything was bright sunshine, I had everything I wanted and needed, that helped me forget all the worlds trash they threw at me. I started having problems with my mail. I was getting calls and wondered where my mail was going. I received a letter with a summary of money sent to me, which I never received. I started making phone calls and found the amount was three thousand dollars. Who could take that much money from someone before they would find out? They had to be getting the mail. I told the people I didn't receive that money I was supposed to get, and I had to find out why. How could I find out what has been going on? I made calls and found out some one owned a home in my name and a nice car. The home had all new furniture in it, and I'm living from pay check to pay check, how could this be? Like I said, someone is watching and waiting to get what you have. I found out where that person lived and wanted to meet her. I know that sounds crazy, but I had to know. I drove to her home or my home in name only. I stayed in my car and just looked at that lovely home; I'm just in a rented house. I had to make up something so I pretended to be a building inspector. She let me in; I walked around looking at how I was living. She had very expensive taste, just like I wanted to live. I wondered why I couldn't get this and she's pretending to be me and living better than me. I made up some papers to make it look like I was a building inspector and said it was over and walked out to my car. "Isn't that some shit, I'm living good or she is." I started to drive back home and began to make phone calls. She must pay for this, and I wanted answers as to how this could happen. She had stolen my identity and was living better than me. I was told that this was going to be something I was going to have to fight and prove that she is not me. The police were called and she went to jail. I was called to come to court and I just looked at her. She didn't do it alone, she had help, but she would not tell me who helped her. She said, "At least all the bills are paid up and I never got behind." I said, "But you're not me and why did you do this?" She said to the judge, "Well she had good credit and I didn't." I couldn't believe that, I walked out of court shaking my head. Now I'm going after the things they let her get, it's was time for that change. She has me owing house payments and car payments. I had to get a lawyer to get this stuff off me. Then I knew why I couldn't get things, she had me looking like I had a lot, they weren't going to give me more anymore until the other things were paid off. The lawyer said this was going to mess me up for some time. She's going to pay for this. Every time my name came up, all that credit she made came up, years of mess I've got to go through. I told the lawyer I wanted everything given to me that she got in my name. He had the nerve to say he didn't think that could be done. I said, "What, it's in my name?" Today I sat back and looked at this life, some of it sucked and the other part is crazy. We have a beach where I live and I go there from time to time to get some peace and think about things. I got drunk and went there. I was so drunk, I wanted to get in the water to cool off, but I didn't make it to the water, because someone was waking me up. I had passed out in the sand, someone asked, "Lady, are you okay?" It was morning, the sun was shining into my eyes; I must have been there five hours. Thank the lord for surrounding me with good people who watches out for me. Now I can go home and see that nothing has changed. I had been a drunken mess, and what did it change? Have you ever done anything so dumb? I bet if you ask someone who knows you, they would say yes. I started getting calls from some man I didn't know, but he kept calling and I wouldn't answer the phone. Then a female called and asked me what I was doing with her man. That was some of the little things that people kept on doing to me, still trying to make me fret, but I've been through this before. I felt numb and kept going on with my life. I knew they watched to see what I would do, I tried hard to shake them, but they kept messing with me. I didn't trust anyone and everyone said I was acting strange. When I went to places, I spotted people following me, every time it was the same folks. One day this person was following me and I had just about enough. I quickly stopped and the car went around me. I turned and ended up behind him. I had turned on a dead-end street and there was nowhere to go, so he had to turn around. I started driving following him, he drove faster and so did I, faster and faster behind him. He acted like a scared rabbit, as he drove faster, every time he turned, I would make the same turn. I began to laugh as we were playing cat and mouse. The faster he was trying to get away from me; he was making scary actions, and almost hitting cars trying to get away from me. I honked the horn and drove faster, and then I stopped as he drove off almost hitting another car. I yelled, "Stop messing with me, stop it," but I knew they would put another trail on me. I said what they wanted, was I missing something, what did they want from me and where did they think I was going? Sometimes people don't want you to be anything, and when they see that you are doing something, they try to stop you from doing it, because you will outshine them. That's sad, because everything you do makes them look bad. They would even show up at my funeral, crying and pretending to love me, but under their breath they are spitting on me and glad I'm gone. I never understood why they were so evil, coming to your house to see what you got. Hate you and smile all in your face, but don't want you to have a bread crumb. Those were the things that kept me away from some people. Once a person shows me their true colors and how they really are, I try to stay away from them. I guess they think I was trying to act like I was better, but I never felt like that; they did. I let people make me feel a bit strange, I didn't really know what I was supposed to feel. No one told me what to feel, so I had so many things going on in my head, what was I to do? If a child is not taught anything, how were they going to know? I have found that the way that you are raised has a huge impact on how you live your life. Be careful and know your children are an extension of their parents. They may do things a little different, but they still are you; if you leave it up to someone else, they will be like them. After all those years, they found a child I used to keep. The last time I saw her, she was two years old. I was so attached to her; I kept her like she was my own child. Her mom was my friend; we became friends after a lot of conversations. One day she came to my home with my husband's cousin, right away I didn't like her, because she had no manners. She was the type of person who would fart and think nothing of it. She put her feet on my couch Indian style, mom always taught me to keep your feet off the furniture. She would go into my fridge and in my cabinets, she had no home training. I was always telling her off, then one day I asked her what her problem was and she told me she was adopted. She said the family she was with didn't take the time to teach her anything; they just wanted the check they got because they needed it to live. They didn't care when she ran away with a man. I told her to try and make peace with them; because maybe she has done some things that have made them angry with her. She seemed so rebellious, but she called and her step mom said some very nasty things. I felt sorry for her. She started to cry, her mom didn't like people who were not like her. She told her to get herself cleaned and get a D and C and she could live in her house again. Poor folks were nasty and dirty to her and her family, because they had money. Her mom felt like she must have sexually transmitted disease that only poor people contract. She told me she was living under a bridge in our hometown. The subway ran no more and homeless people started living down there. That's where she lived; she sold herself to have something to eat. When my husband cousin named Jim saw her on the streets, she would go places with him, he fed her and sometimes she spent the night with him. I told her to tell him that she was homeless, and right away he moved her in, it was right next door to us. Every day she came over and talked with me, we had coffee and I grew to like her. After a few months, she said she was going to have a baby. He was happy; he loved her and tried to give her a good home. I started to make clothes again to make some extra money, and that allowed me to meet many people. We met this lady who was a babysitter. Joy wanted to go to work and try and fix her broken life. After the baby was born, and she got well, and she needed someone to keep her baby. She had one little girl, who was the love of our lives. One day, Jim told me she had left in the middle of the night, she didn't take the baby and he wanted to see if she was back under that bridge, but he couldn't find her. He called the police and no one could find her. She never told me she was unhappy, I guess I wasn't really her friend, how could I be? She ran away and left that baby, Jim worked something out with the babysitter. When I got off my part time job, I would keep her when he needed someone to keep her; I would keep her when I wasn't working. She missed two birthdays and a half of a year. Joy came back to take her baby from that babysitter. Jim was so hurt. He found out she had been in Florida with seasonal bean pickers. The seasonal work ended and they were to take her where she lived. They really lived a poor life, why would she do that? She felt like she loved that new guy and would follow him anywhere, but he didn't want her child to come with them. When she left the baby the first time, she felt like a bad mom and came back this time to take her back. Years went by and we didn't hear anything, until one day my friend Jim told me a social worker in Florida contacted him. She told him his child was in foster care and asked if he would sign her over. He told her he wanted his child and that the mom had taken her years ago. They said he would have to come get her. He asked how long would it be, and he told her he would have to take vacation time. When the social worker called back, she said she could put his child on a plane with another social worker and she would have to be picked up. Jim was there to pick her up. She didn't know any of us. She only had a book of pictures her mom gave her, and that's how she recognized who we were. That child must have been mistreated. The social worker said her mom was very sick and was in a mental hospital and the county took her kids. We didn't get the real story, but he got her back. Jim was now married to some lady I didn't know. The child went to their house, I didn't see her much, but I would hear plenty. Jim's new wife was abusing his child and her own children, and those poor children went through hell. His child was supposed to be having a better life, but she had a wicked step mother instead. When he went to work, she would verbally abuse her and then she started hitting her. That went on for a while; she was living like her mom all over again. One day she started to fight back, she had enough. When she hit her, she ran and told her dad. He didn't know what to do, but he did want his family together. She wanted his daughter to leave, so she left and went to live with her older sister until she was able to get her own job and her own house. But that kind of stuff messes your mind up. I got a chance to see her when she was all grown up now. She was a lovely young lady. I was proud of her; she made her life good even if she came up bad. Things were getting bad all around me. My friend Rosa was in a bad accident and I rushed to see her. She had broken bones in her back; they said they didn't know if she would walk again. She was taking it like a trooper, she talked to me when I came into the room and it took everything in me not to cry. They were going to do surgery on her back to fuse her bones together; I knew that this was in God hands. While I was at the hospital, this nurse was very rude to me. I didn't know her; maybe she was having a bad day, when she came in the room she bumped into me. When they brought Rosa back in the room after surgery, I waited for her to wake up. In came that same nurse, giving me dirty looks and being very rude. Rosa opened her eyes and gave me that big smile; I knew she would be all right. When I got home my phone rang and someone hung up, this went on about four days. I told Rosa someone was calling and hanging up on me. We tried to find out who it was, but just like everything else in my life, there was always someone out to mess me up. At that point I just let the phone rang when I saw that number. When a new number came up I answered and said hello. There was a woman on the other line who asked, "How long have you been seeing my man?" I asked, "Who is this?" She said, "You know who this is." I said, "I don't know you." She said she got my number out of Rosa's record at the hospital. I said,

"You must be that nurse." She said, "Yes I am." I told her I didn't know her or her man. She told me his name and I said, "I work with him, but I'm not going out with him, he's a co-worker. She went on to tell me how he was keeping up with me and the information about where I lived and where my relatives lived. He was spying on me and I didn't know it. She said he had pictures of me in many places. I felt a lump in my throat. Why was he following me? The next day I went into work and looked him up. I asked him why he was following me. He told me someone hired him to keep up with me and he had partners. I told him I was going to call the police. By that time, he had removed his stuff from his girlfriend's house, and that would make me look like I was lying. I called the hospital and told them that the nurse told me she got my number from Rosa's hospital records. They checked the number she called. He called me and told me to take back my story I told the hospital staff. I asked, "Tell me who paid you to spy on me?" He said he couldn't and I told him I couldn't take back the story that I told while I was in the hospital. The nurse ended up being fired from the hospital. After she put him out he called me. I told him I would call the police if he called me again. Was there something I saw or ran across? I was racking my brain, because I didn't know who had him watching and following me. I had vacation time off work and I took it. I didn't want to leave the house. I started to check my home, maybe they had been in my home. They did it before, maybe this time too. Bugs and cameras could look like anything, I didn't know what to look for, but I was looking. Again, I began to wonder if they had been inside my home. I started to wonder if they had put anything in my food, maybe my children have eaten something. What was I going to do about all of this? Those evil people have spent years trying to destroy my life, but I won't let them. This must end, even if it takes everything I have in me. Then someone started sending messages to my friends and family telling them all sorts of things. My family and friends came and told me about the messages. Those secret messages become clear to light. They couldn't find out exactly who it came from. Everybody was mad at each other because of these. A lot of letters were real nasty, they would but who did it? It had to be someone smart, because they were set up so you couldn't tell where they really came from. One thing it did do was get all my folks talking again, and that was a good thing. I couldn't believe some of the nasty things that were said, but you don't really know people like you think you do. My past has made it hard for me to trust anyone, and it's so hard living like this, but what am I to do? A group of us got together and the talks began, I mean all twenty of us had been molested. All in one family, here are some of their stories. This is Missy. One night as she slept, she felt hands touching her; it was one of her cousins. He forced himself on her, how nasty that must have felt; someone in her family and did she tell anybody about that? She should have, but she didn't until now and she's all messed up in the head. That was why she is gay; she never wanted a man to hurt her again. The next story was my sister, that one really hurt me. My sister told how her and her brother carried on for years in a relationship. They said they didn't want to trust anyone they didn't know, and they felt like that was the way. Thank the Lord there were no children between them, but then we did have another in law who had a child with each other, and how do you hide this? There are generations of sexual abuse in this family. One girl was sold to a man by her mother. Men would come into the trailer and her mother would take the money and send them into the bedroom. This went on until the girl had enough and ran away. She didn't have a way to take care of herself, and she started to do the only thing her mother had taught her, how sad. There are so many children being sexually abused in this world. We must stop these kids from being subjected to this, because those kids are going to be adults and messed up in their judgements; which is clouded by their past. Can you imagine yourself going to one of the people and needing help, and they are the only one to give it to you? No matter how much education a person may have, their personality comes into play in all they do and say, because you can't get away from being you.

CHAPTER NINE – AND THEN THERE WAS JAMES

I was sitting on a park bench when my eyes caught the eye of the finest man I had seen in a long time. He had the nerves to sit down on my bench; I wanted to be alone so I could think. When he sat down, it made me wonder why. Who was he? I couldn't help noticing his big brown eyes. At first, we didn't say anything. Then he finally said, "Hi my name is James." I told him my name and we began to talk. I could hardly look in his eyes, they were mesmerizing. He asked me if I came to the park a lot, I said "Yes, I do come to this park a lot." "Do you come here a lot also?" I asked. We talked for a long time and time slipped by. I told him I had to go and he said he'll see me there again. He didn't ask for my number, but I wanted to give it to him. I couldn't talk as I looked in his eyes. I didn't go back to the bench in the park until Wednesday, two weeks later and he was there. I said, "Hi James" as our eyes met and he asked, "Are you in love?" I asked, "Why do you want to know, are you in love?" He said, "Not yet, but I plan on being in love soon." Then I asked, "What does that mean," as I looked at him, he kissed me and we began kissing each other, and it felt good to me. Then I said, wait a minute, I don't even know him and pushed him away, but he seemed like he could charm the skin off a snake. I started to push him away, but my heart wanted to keep kissing him. He smiled and said, "Yes I think I'm going to be in love soon." We started dating; I had been without a man for a while. During the weekend, we would go to the next town to be together. He would always say he worked in our town all week and he liked to get away because people would see him and want to talk about business. We had a very passionate affair. After not having a man in a long time, this was just what I desired. He knew how to please a woman, "I think I'm in love." I didn't ask him many questions; I just loved everything that was going on at that time. He filled my life with so much joy. I should have wondered why we always left town when we would spend the entire weekend together. We had to be out of town James told me. He said he had a lot of business in town and he didn't want to run into people he worked with and we had to leave, so his business partners wouldn't mess with him while we were having our time together; I believed him. One night James said, "Let's stay in town tonight, get something to eat and go to a local hotel." We could have gone to my house, but he said he wanted the hotel. We stopped to get something to eat, this time I drove my car. We were inside the place getting our order, in walked this woman who looked at James and said, "Hi James." I didn't think anything about it, because he was a business man, but he continued talking. Our order came up and he paid for it. I started to walk towards the door as he continued to talk to her, and she said, "I thought you were out of town on business." He acted like he didn't know me. Then she asked him, "So what time are you coming home?" I turned around and looked at him. She said, "You should have told me, I would have cooked dinner and the kids would love to see you." I didn't say a word, I couldn't, and my heart fell to my feet. I just walked out the door, tears filled my eyes. I got into my car; I sat there and began to cry. I couldn't move for that moment. Who was she, was she his wife, is that the reason we always left town? I was so much in love and so much in pain. I couldn't think, but I started my car and drove home, I wondered if I got caught up once again. He didn't call me until the end of the week, the phone rang and it was him. I answered and said, "James, why, why did you do this to me; to us?" He said, "I can't make any excuses, but I really do love you, I love you so much, I could hardly talk to you." I heard him cry as he tried to talk, he said, "I'm so sorry, I never meant to hurt you, we fell so deeply in love and I didn't want it to stop." I heard him say, "I'm not going to lie to you, she is my wife, but we've had a few hard times, that night she walked up on us, we were fighting." He even thanked me for not making a scene. He said, "I know that's not helping the way you feel." I told him "Like I said, we fell in love so deeply and I just didn't want to let you go, we were so happy, but I know I have to let you go. I can no longer see you, I told you when we first met I didn't want to mess with anyone's husband, because it was done to me, and you still walked me right into this. Don't call me anymore, even if I still love you, time will heal my heart and you will only be in my memories, good bye." I knew in my heart that was a lie. I hung up and cried harder than I ever had in my life. James, I loved, or so I thought I found my true love. It's going to take a long time to get over this. He filled my life with so much love and I felt at peace with him. Now days I found myself looking off into space, I lost that person that I used to be. For months, I was leaning on him, he was there and he gave me so much joy. It took all I had to forget about how nasty people were to me and how I was being watched and my property torn up. Where do I go from here? I called one of my friends and said, "Let's go have a drink." We met at the club. I drank and drank until I couldn't stand up. My friend Millie said, "Damn, you are drunk; let me help you out of here." She and another co-worker helped me out of the club. I couldn't walk on my own, they got two other people and the four of them carried me to the car. Millie said she would take me home, but I couldn't leave my car there, in the morning it would be towed away. Then one person drove me home and the other one followed us. When we pulled up to my house, everything I drank came back up; I opened the door just in time. I had just made a fool of myself, trying to drink away that love, but in my mind, I knew I couldn't do that. Millie asked me what was wrong. I told her that James was married and I've been a fool. She said some women would still see him, even if he was married. I started crying while still heaving all over. They took me into the house, helped me clean myself up, made me some coffee and we talked until the morning light. It was nice to have good friends, without my friends, I don't know what I would have done. Maybe I would have been insane by now. They stood by me through thick and thin, and I loved them dearly. Most of them had been there when I had my children and when I went through everything I had with my husband. They were there when I got married and through all my break ups, I'm at the point where I know how I wanted to be treated by a man. Some say this is so tragic, but who could I trust? Are there any people that I can trust? My children were coming home to see me and I had to pull myself together. I went out to buy food so we could have meals. I couldn't let them know that I was in pain. They had not met James and I was glad about that. I wanted to take the time to get to know him first. While my children were away at school, that gave me a lot of time on my hands. As I drove to the store, I began to think to myself, "Was he a set up or did he care for me, or was it just some kind of sick joke?" I went into the market and saw an old friend. He tried to talk to me but I kept right on walking. He walked up to me and asked, "What's wrong with you?" I said, "I'm sorry, it's nothing you did, I got a lot on my mind." He said, "Give me your number; I would like to talk to you." I gave it to him and went on with my shopping. I was getting excited about seeing my children. They were coming in from three different parts of the country. Being with them would take my mind off other things. I called every family member I could, to have them over for dinner. My doorbell rang, it was my oldest son. He walked in looking just like his dad. He had his girlfriend with him, that was the first time I met her and she seemed nice. The doorbell rang again; it was a lot of the family who came along with Pissy ass Chris. He was always drunk and pissing on himself. I said, "No Chris, let me pull out my pad for you, you're not pissing on my stuff this time." My girls came in asking if they could help with the food. The dinner went well. We all began to talk about our lives. Oh, no I didn't want to tell them about mine. Everyone was laughing and having a good time. They asked me what I was doing while my kids were away at school. Then the doorbell rang, the bell saved me. It was Joel, he came by to see our daughter Jolina, and he knew she was coming home on her break. He had been trying to get back with me, but I tried to stay away from him. He would show up when he felt like it, and if I had people over, he would just join in like who asked him, not me. At one time, I cared deeply for Joel, but he was too much of a player for me. We did have a good time, we were passionate and we had good sex, everywhere at that moment in time. I was drinking and down for whatever. For six years, he didn't see or take care of Jolina. I was her mom and dad, to her; all those days and nights she was sick, and I stayed up with her. I held her when she didn't feel well about the world. But Joel was a very good sex partner, that's all he was good for. He didn't mind doing what it took to please me. He gave his love all over town; I was afraid that I may catch something, like AIDS or any other STD. You can't make a player a settled man. I needed someone that was mine, a husband and Joel wasn't that man. When I busted him with that woman, he told me she was one of five and I was the fifth. He said he liked something about each one of us, like I was one of his sweet candies in his candy box. That's what he called me, a sweet piece of candy. He was another snake in the grass, but I liked what he did to me at that time. One day I went to his house and there was woman's jacket in the living room. I guess he didn't notice it because she wasn't supposed to be there. She came out of the room just before we got undressed to go to bed. Joel was surprised, they started yelling and cursing at each other. I stood there and Joel told her he had to take me home because he brought me there. She became madder and said some old dumb stuff; I told her she doesn't know me, but I would knock her into next week. I said, "Come take me home, you can handle this when you come back." He told her to leave and took away the keys; he said he'll talk to her later. She got in her car and drove off fast. I wanted to hit Joel on the head, but I wasn't going to be pulled into doing that. I didn't want to fight; I had enough of that with my husband. She called him on the phone, cursed him out and told me he was not going to mess with me anymore. While she was talking that trash, I decided to keep having sex with Joel. Like I told her, he doesn't want to settle down with no one. While I played around with Joel that night, we got drunk, took off the condom and four weeks later, we had Jolina. Jolina was the joy of my life. He wanted me to end my child's life, but I didn't want to, I always felt that would-be murder. One day he came over to my house with that bitch in his car. I asked, "Why did you bring her here this Joel, get her away from my house." He said, "She wanted to know what was going on between me and you." I said, "Bitch please you're going to get it if you don't leave me alone, Joel get her from in front of my house now!" I was glad Jolina wasn't there to see or hear what happened. I was so mad; I went back into the house and slammed the door. About a week went by before I heard from Joel. I asked him what he wanted; he said he was through with her. I told him to get away from my house now. That was the last time I saw him for two years. His child was well taken care of and I loved our child. Now here he comes like the proud dad to see her while she was home from school. She told me he had been sending her money and care boxes of things while she was at school. He tried to make himself look good. I went from heart break to being pissed off. In a few short hours, Joel managed to pull me down a little bit more. But I've got to get it together, my kids are home and it was time to party. I put on some of that ole school music and we sang and laughed most of the night away, dinner was good too. Talking about old times does make it all worth what we've all been through. I said, "I'm sleepy and off to bed, everyone that wants to stay find a place to sleep, everyone but Joel, beat it." Everyone laughed as I pointed to the door, he left and I was off to bed, tomorrow will be a new day. I woke up to the smell of bacon and eggs, my youngest son Thomas the chef was cooking. I got up and headed down where everyone was waiting for me. We all sat down for breakfast, as we sat down we began to talk. Thomas was the chief; he started telling everyone how nasty people are and was always in his business. I heard a knock at the door, it was Joel. He asked, "Can I get some food this morning or do I have to go to the corner eatery?" I said, "Come on in Joel." We talked and laughed for the rest of the morning, Joel got a call and left. My phone rang and someone on the other end said, "Nice family you have." I said, "Stop it Joel," but as I listened to the voice it wasn't him. He said, "We are still watching you," I acted like it was the wrong number. My kids knew it bothered me and they asked who it was. I said, "Wrong number," and tried to get them to talk about their experiences at school. They all went to different colleges, their stories were different, but they were happy and that's all I ever wanted them; just to be happy. Thomas had a job as a cook, but he was still in school getting his education as well. He said he was being treated like he didn't know anything. I knew when he cooked for me he was very creative and folks were jealous of the things he made for me. He made good grades in school and he maintained a 3.5 grade point average. All his class mates were always amazed by the dishes that he would create, and some of them became very jealous. They decided that they were going to find a way to make him look bad. They started brain storming and they all agreed on putting the wrong ingredients in one of his recipes. When he went to display how to cook this recipe in front of the professor for a test, he recognized that he didn't have the right ingredients and that caused him to flunk the test. Thomas told me he had some good friends who got wind of it and told him. Then Thomas was going to prepare the dish (Coq au vin). That was a soup made with red wine. Someone was going to pour in more wine than needed, but Thomas left the wine out. Some lady started to talk to him so they could pour in the wine. His plan was to win the mark, so after she poured in about the right amount, his friend told him to turn around fast to stop her from pouring. He told her he saw her and she acted like she was just getting the aroma of the soup in her nose as she walked away. Thomas finished his soup and the master chief came around, they wanted him to tell Thomas his soup was bad and had too much wine, but he kissed his fingers and said, "Magnificent." This time all their heads dropped, Thomas was on top, but then he knew he had to watch his back and his food. Maybe I have not trusted people in my life time, but how could I trust anyone. They say you must trust someone, but I need to check them out good. Take time to know them and their ways before I could call them my true friend. Marlene was my oldest daughter; she told me she encountered haters. Too many females don't like each other, for no reason at all. Sometimes they think you look better or dress better than them. Silly little things females go through, unless you have the right friends. Jolina told me she left her dorm room to go to class, when she came back all her clothes were gone, I mean not one piece of clothing was left in her room. She went to the guard's office and reported them missing. He looked at the video and saw her so called friends taking her clothes. He got on the loud speaker and the whole school heard him say, "All of the haters on the third floor, building H house, put back all the clothes that came from room #315 back now or the Dean will come see you and you will not continue this semester, you have only 15 minutes." Jolina stood with the guard and looked at the camera while the girls took her clothes back into the room. When the last girl came out, he told Jolina to go back to her room and don't even say anything about her stuff. He told her he would be watching and the other guards too, so in the future this will not happen again. She said her clothes were folded all nice and neat. Those are some things you go through as you grow up and get older, you have haters. While I talked to my kids, I got another phone call. It was the same voice, he told me he heard everything we talked about and repeated it. I know the kids saw the look on my face, and asked me what was wrong. This time I had recorded him and his message, they were highly upset. I said, "This is what I've been going through, and I can't find out how they hear us. Everyone started taking things apart to see if they could find the bug, or maybe it's more than one. We looked in lamps, the phone, the TV, and every plant I had. My son asked, "Have you gotten any new gifts lately?" I said, "Yes that tree you sent me," he said he didn't send me a tree. Then he pulled it apart and found a small hearing piece. He pulled it off and smashed it. They found one in the lamps, stuck there on the bottom and I never looked there. Everything I got for Christmas and presents sent to me, we found so many bugs. But why were they doing this to me and my children, I wanted to know. I said once I walked in on two people, inside one of my job's office and saw them having sex on the desk. They were both married to someone else. Even when people were stealing gas from the company cars, I saw and heard a lot in my years on those jobs. Sometimes at lunch there were sex frenzies. A lot of wives thought their husbands were working, but they were having sex every place they could find, but I wasn't the only one who witnessed those things. I wondered if others were being watched like that or would they tell? I was so sick of all those things going on. People had no lives if they took the time out of their day to try and tear up another human being's soul, why do they continue to try to destroy my life? They thought they could cause me to hate them, but I felt sorry for all those folks who felt they needed to try to tear apart my life. They tried so hard to make everyone hate me. They told people that didn't even know me horrible things about me and my children, and the horrific part about it was that people believed them. I have always felt way about all of that, and that's why I decided that if someone chooses to hate me go ahead, I can't make them love me. I just felt sorry for those who wanted everyone to hate me. I've done nothing but loved everyone I met. Let me say this right now, because I was not like them, they tore me down anyway they could. I went into work, they were getting on my nerves, as I walked to the building I saw my co-worker named George, he asked me to help him and I told him to stop playing. I had just lost a friend of mine a few weeks ago, and he's playing like that; it wasn't funny. I kept walking and again he said, "Help me." I said, "I'll have them call 911." When I got inside the building, I asked someone to call 911 for George. I found out he had a heart attack. We were all upset because this has been happening too often. I then found out that four coworkers that I used to work with at that job have also passed away, what was going on? One of the friends came by and he was partying, he never drank alcohol before, and I wanted to know why now, but he wouldn't tell me. One day he wanted to try it. We were looking for him and no one knew where he had gone, they called for him for more than an hour, but he didn't answer. Then someone found him two streets over, dead inside his vehicle. He drank so much his heart stopped. I cried so hard, he was my best friend. People thought we were going together, but he was like my big brother. I told them to go call his family, before; they were only going to call his wife, but I went by their house to give his wife a ride to the hospital. As we talked, she began to scream and cry. I got her to the hospital and she had to be rolled in a wheelchair. Poor lady, the news just broke her heart. I stayed with her until her family came to be with her. I went home; I could hardly see the road because I was crying so hard, but I was glad that I made it home safely. There was always something going on at that job. I couldn't help but wonder because there was never a dull moment when I was working there. I went out on the road to do my route, when I got back to my car; it was in shambles and papers pulled out like they had been looking for something. I went into the office to tell them. They called me into the manager's office, and she asked me if I had a gun. I said, "What!" She asked again, "Well do you?" I told her I was going to call the police because no one had the right to go into my car. She said she didn't know about that, but a note was left saying I had a gun. No gun was inside my car, but this must have been someone that I felt was close to me running their mouth. I may have said something about a gun, but why would they want to hurt me? My guess is that these people were not my friends, and they knew who broke into my car. I thought I knew who it was, but I didn't say anything. On the way home, I stopped to wash my car, I said, "This time I was smarter then whoever tried to steal my gun. The one thing that these people failed to recognize was that they were the ones who made me get a gun because I didn't know who was trying to harm me and my kids. I stopped at the store to get something, when I came out; the whole side of my car was keyed, I mean all down one side. People were standing around and no one would tell me who did it. I saw a vehicle pulling off that had our company's logo on the side. All the vehicles have numbers and I saw it, but no one would tell me if they did it. I felt like people were completely oblivious to the fact that when they try to hurt me; they were hurting my children as well. Everything that went on inside or outside of my house affected my children. I knew that there weren't any kids that were bold enough to do something like this to my car; I knew that it was some adults that were responsible for keying my car. I was told, no matter what I get, they will destroy it. I felt like every time I started making some progress in my life, something always happens and it sets me back from being able to move forward with my life. I started to get depressed, and I felt like I was a failure, So much hate in this world, why? There's room for us all, no one is bumping into anyone. Personalities are always clashing, someone thinks you're too loud, someone thinks you're too quiet, you're too big, too small, too black, too white, too smart, too dumb, or too everything. Why not just let people be whoever they want to .be? Like Rodney King said, "Can't we all just get along?" Why do people waste their time being evil and malicious towards one another? I have had so much of my property destroyed and damaged that I feel like I am going to lose my mind. I don't understand what they feel like they are accomplishing. I'm not mad, I just feel sorry for them, because they can't see past their own selfishness and wicked ways. I guess they were trying to drive me crazy, but it only made me stronger. I got a call from one of my friends, she asked me to meet her at another friend's house. When I pulled up there, I saw a U-Haul truck and men were loading it. Our friends' man was leaving her, she was screaming, "Please don't leave me, please." I was horrified to see her begging so hard, as he walked around picking up his things. She was crying her eyes out and he just had a blank look on his face, to me this was crazy. She loved him so much that he had her begging for him not to leave, I finally slapped her and I said, "Pull yourself together, he's letting you know he doesn't want you anymore; let him go." She kept crying and running after him, as he walked to the door one more time, she fell to the floor, grabbed his leg, and he started trying to walk away and she wouldn't let go of his leg so he began dragging her to make her let go. She was begging him to please not leave her. I felt like I could understand how she was feeling inside, but I couldn't act like while everyone was watching. Nothing else meant anything to her that day except him leaving, how sad. She didn't want to live without him. I was very mad at her and I told her, "Your life is yours, you need to claim it, don't let a man make you feel weak and helpless because you have so much to live for, and you have to move on with your life, not just for you but for your children as well. I was so glad her children were at her mom's, because they would have seen this mess going on. I felt sorry for her because I knew that she was hurting so I let her know that she could always come and talk to me when she needed a friend. He left the state and she said she was going to follow him. I told her it was a bad move on her part, because he didn't want her. I said, "You can't make anyone care, and there is no amount of sex or money that can change a person's feelings, that only sets you up to get used." Well, she didn't listen to me and two weeks later she left. When found him in another state she looked him up, and he had gotten married to a woman he brought with him from our town. She found that out when she went to his mother's house. She still wanted to see him. He went to his mother's house and told her direct, he didn't want her, no matter what she said she would do for him, he didn't want her anymore. With her heartbroken, she called me, I said, "Girl come home now, you're making a fool of yourself." She got on a bus and headed back home. When she got back home we had lunch and talked about just letting it go. I know we all have our own way of letting go. I was there for her if she needed to vent, cry or even yell and cuss, because we were friends. I wanted to call all my friends together for a meeting of the minds. We had all been through some things and I felt like this would be a good exercise for all of us. This time I got to pick the place to meet at for girls' night, and we were out on the town again. We had a nice dinner and then we went to a cabin. We all started to vent, played old slow music, drank, cried, and talked. That was our way of getting things off our chest, we talked, and I think that this was the one thing that men didn't understand about females, because we always like to talk things out until we can rationalize it in our minds. My friend Marsha has been very distant lately because of her recent break up. She walked in on her man having sex with another man. She couldn't tell us because she was embarrassed, just like anyone of us would be. The man that she fell in love with and gave her heart too, ended up being guy. They weren't married, but she felt like they would be soon. They had put together a beautiful relationship, and it looked fine on the outside. She noticed he just wasn't attracted to her when they were home, but around friends, he seemed to be so in love with her. That was only to fool everyone on the outside. He told her not to ever talk about their love life to any of her friends, or he would walk out. She had been finding signs all around the house. She found tickets to all male strip shows and gay pictures on his computer. In her heart, she kept saying, "No he can't be," she knew, but didn't want to lose him. He was never hers, you can't change someone; they must change themselves. She went to visit her mom in Portland, OR, when she came back into town, she found more tickets and that let her know he was gay. About a month later she went to see her mom again, because she was sick, but this time it was short and she wanted to come home early because her mom seemed all right now. This is what happened, I'm not going to gay bash, but I told her she should have left then, and she wouldn't have seen what she saw. When she opened the door to the house, she heard sounds of love making coming from her bedroom. She started to cry and she couldn't believe it. She slowly looked inside the room and he was in the very act of sex with another man. She said she began to scream, "No, no, no, oh no." He slowly looked at her and calmly said, "You should have called to tell me you were on your way home." But why would she tell him, she wanted to surprise him. She brought him a gift back from Portland, something she felt he would love, but she saw what he loved with her own eyes. He told his lover, "Get up baby, go home and I'll call you when I take care of this mess." He called his relationship with her a mess. She stood there not knowing what to say. He told her to pack her things and get out; he told her to get what was hers in their home and just go. He had made up his mind that he was gay. That broke her down, and she just walked out and came to my house and cried. She didn't tell anyone until all the girls decided to get together for a girl's night. We were all there to vent because this year had been very challenging for all of us. Then she said she didn't know if she could trust any man right now, but I told her not to give up yet, because her life will get better; don't give up. But then she died. The funeral was planned. She looked like she was sleeping at peace. None of us said anything to him, only to the kids and her family. One down and how many more? We were all beginning to get sick in our bodies; some had high blood pressure, headaches, and depression. Then there was my friend Shelisa. You knew when she came in the place, she was loud and very tall, and we called her Lee Lee. She was a bit country. We met Shelisa at work. She was new in town so we all tried to help her out as much as we could. She was very country, and she didn't have a clue about the city life. She was from the deep south, and she was always asking questions about how to do this or that. She was a good friend and she would give you the shirt off her back, and then tell you, "Girl I'm so cold," that's how country she was. She thought that if a man smiled at her he was interested in getting to know her. I had to tell her that all he wanted was her pocketbook. She said, "My pocket book doesn't have any money in it." I said, "Girlfriend, it means sex with you and no attachments." Well she messed around and got into a sexual thing with this one man, he was a jackass and he fooled her. Lee Lee told us she was moving in with him, and it was his mom's house. She was working two jobs, and they started taking her money. This man would take her money and give her what he wanted her to have. He would spend her money on the most expensive clothes that he could find. He came from a family that liked to party and drink, so when she did have time off he tried to keep her intoxicated. She would call always call me when she got wasted, and she would always tell me she was having such a good time. She would make it to work every day after being totally drunk the night before. She felt like she was living the life. Every day he would have the tub water warm and waiting, and he would pick her clothes out and lay them on the bed. Well, he should be doing a lot more for her because he didn't have a job. He would always try to butter her up so he could get her money at the end of the week. Meanwhile he was playing with other women too, but she was too blind to see. He knew when she fell asleep at night he could sneak out and leave. He would get her so smashed and she would fall asleep, and that's when he would sneak out and run the streets because he knew that she would sleep all night. Everyone would see him out except her. She didn't believe it because in the morning when she got up, he was there some place in the house. One night she had to see it for herself. When he poured her drinks, she dumped them in a vase and told him she was going to bed, well later she heard and saw him leave. The next morning, she acted like everything was alright as she was going to work. He always tried to get smart with me because I was her friend, but I would give it right back to him. He tried to cuss at me, but I would cuss him out every time he said anything to me. I couldn't stand the sight of him, always walking around like he was a pimp. She saw how nasty he was with her own eyes so now she can't deny what other people were saying about him. You would not believe what Lee Lee told me next. She said he brought a lady home because he wanted to have a threesome. He thought she was country green and told her it would make him love her more, because he desired that. Before he got home with the lady, Lee Lee had plans of having a foursome, and she wasn't as green as he thought she was. Lee Lee had a man in the closet, as they began to have sex with that lady; he came out the closet right in front of her and he started making love to Lee Lee. He couldn't say a word when she asked him, "This will make us love each other right?" He had a blank look on his face and yelled, "All right everybody out," but not before she had her fun; green turned into red. Lee Lee looked at him and asked, "Now do you love me more?" He became enraged when she asked him that question, "You've been cheating?" She said, "Just before you came home with her I was having sex with him because I found out just how nasty you were two can play that game; so, what do you want to do?" Then she said, "From now on I'll take care of the bills, I think I should because I live here, that's only until I find my own place." His mom told her everything about her own son; because she was too nice of a lady to let her son take advantage of her like that. He tried to make up, but it was broken and she wouldn't sleep with him anymore. A few weeks went by and she moved out and invited all the ladies to come over for her house warming party, and we partied all night long until the sun came up. As time went by, she became a whore and she was bringing home all types of guys. We tried to talk to her, because she was on a road of destruction. She didn't care what they looked like or what they had. She tried to drink her pain away and make herself nasty as her man made her feel. She was only here to tell her story, because she had turned her life around, she finally saw all eyes were watching her and she was looking very bad, but we loved our Lee Lee. Then there was my friend Ashaha. She came to this country with so many dreams, but she had no money. She fell into whatever was going on around her. She had been raped much of her life, and she was an outcast in her homeland. She wanted to make a better life for herself, so she sold herself to get to this country. When she got to this country she continued to sell herself to every man that was willing to pay her for her services. She was begging in front of grocery stores before we met, I told her I would help her get an honest job. We filled out several applications and she finally got hired, but the job didn't pay her that much money. She told me that as a child she didn't have any shoes, and she would always have to wear dirty clothes. She said all her family would drink dirty water, and everyone was always sick. She said her family put her out in the streets to turn tricks so that she could make money to feed the family. When she was seven she found out just how nasty men could be. How could they do that to a child? They did all kinds of things to her. She grew up being a seasoned prostitute. When she met us, some man was her pimp, he didn't like the way we talked her out of tricking for him. When he tried to hit her we all jumped on him and beat him until he was senseless, and then we would call the police. We tried not to kill him, but we made sure that he wouldn't put his hands on her at all anymore. She moved far away from where he hung out at so that she never had to see his face again. Ashaha was a very nice lady, but she had a hard time trying to stay away from prostitution. We tried to tell her to get a good man and we thought that she was trying to change, but she was still selling out in the streets tricking for money. One of our friends moved near her and said Ashaha was running men in and out of her house all day and night and throughout the weekend. We all thought that she needed to seek mental help because she was going crazy. We were all crying in the cabin because we had all been through so much physical and mental abuse. This woman grew up being used and didn't feel right unless she was abused. She never had any children and maybe she needed someone that she could truly love and give her heart too. Then there was a knock on the cabin door, it was Mary's husband, she couldn't go anyplace unless he showed up. This is my friend Mary. She was a very disturbed woman, her nerves were so bad, and she would sometimes pee on herself because of her anxiety. We had to almost force her to come out of the house, and she had to tell him where we were going to be. We asked her not to tell him, but she was afraid that if she didn't then he would get upset with her. He puts his hands on her all the time, and now there was going to be trouble. We were all worked up about the abuse we had gone through. He banged on the door and we told him to go away. Then she opened the door for him, we said we were going to call the police. Soon as he came in Mary and her husband started fighting. I did all I could to stop that mad women from fighting. This was our place and our time; he had no right coming there. The police came and told him to leave, but they told her to go with him, and she did. Mary was getting beat up all the time and she wouldn't call the police. He would gun butt her all the time, she was so dingy, I guess getting hit on the head all the time would do that to a person. One night she ran away from him, that's when she told me about the beatings. He told her that he didn't want me at their house because I was just trying to cause problems between the both, which was not the truth by any means. I did stay away from their home and I only saw her at work, until tonight when I picked her up. I bet he beat her all the way home from the cabin. We all saw the abuse, and it was so sad because we couldn't do anything about it. Like I said, someone is always watching. We all knew something about each other, because we were all nosey, and we would get drunk and talk about our personal life with one another. After we finished at the cabin, we found out later she was found dead in her driveway. He claimed he went to the store and she was lying in the driveway when he came back. They say she was extremely angry when they saw her. We didn't believe it, her poor children. This just broke all our hearts, and we all decided to go home because there was no way that we could stay at the cabin after we found out that our friend was dead. We had to figure out a way to help with nurturing her children for the next couple of days. The funeral was planned. She looked like she was sleeping at peace. None of us said anything to him, only to the kids and her family. One down and how many more? We were all beginning to get sick to our stomach; some had high blood pressure, headaches, and depression. Some of us were crazy or maybe all of us, years of abuse will do that. As days went by, I started feeling so bitter, I didn't tell anyone, but I was mad, why can't people just live and be happy, why was there so much unhappiness in this life? Everybody had something wrong. But then I thought I do know some people that I know are happy. That old couple I know, they are eighty- two years old, and both are the sweetest people I know. They were my aunt and my uncle; they met years ago, when they both were widowed. They had gotten old and needed someone to love. They walked so slow and held hands as they walked and it always made me smile when I saw them. They got married when they were seventy-nine years old. I asked her why she got married now, she told me I'd be surprised at how much they can do with each other. Right now, I needed to smile, because there had been so much pain, laughter is the best therapy. Even though bad things have happened, there have been some joys. Although bad things happen, there is love all around me and no one can take that away from me. God made sure, even though I had haters, I still had love around me. Folks watched me and God watched them. I want to have a relationship that is fulfilling, but it has somehow passed me by. The times I tried, it ended messed up, and one sided love was the story of my life. My husband didn't love or respect me; he walked out and started a new life with another woman that he treated with respect. I think I was not a part of that, even when I tried to make it work. The only benefit that I received from that relationship was my children and I love them until death do us part. He never made me feel loved or needed; he made me feel like the exact opposite underappreciated and used. I talked to my children hoping they would find true love in their lives. My relationships were turmoil, and often-times I would blame myself. I was abused, and because I continued to let it happen it lead me down a path of self-destruction. Drinking like crazy and living promiscuously, now I believe this to be true. I was living fed up because I was fed up. I never found that love; because I didn't know how. I had been used and that's how I allowed men to treat me. Will I ever find that special someone or is it over? I spend my nights alone and can't sleep, longing for someone to cuddle with and love me, talk to me, kiss me and be there for me. This life I'm living is so cold and

bland, I'm living, but what can I do right now when I have other issues
to deal with. Some say go to God with it, somehow, I thought He had
been fed up with my life for years. I went to church, when I came out,
someone had hit my car and ran. I felt numb, did they hit it on purpose
or was it an accident? Whoever it was had left me with another bill to
pay for the damage on my car. It's been this way for years, and I can't
catch them. Why don't they do what's right? Maybe that's why they
did it, to change my mind about things, but they should know by now
this will not stop me, it's been going on for too long; so, I press on and
try to make the best of it. I don't trust very many people, if someone
tried to get to know me, up goes the brick wall. I was told today that I
told someone I was going to kill her; that was another lie to make
people dislike me. I never told anyone that. One day this woman was
in the movies yelling and cussing at me from three seats behind her
and her kids were behind me. She told her kids to kick my seat, I asked
her nicely not to tell them to kick my seat and to stop throwing
popcorn at me. I nicely asked her again to tell them to stop before they
saw their mother get a black eye, and I meant it. She and the kids kept
it up, so I jumped back over the seat and began to tear at that Bitch.
We were all put out, until this day; I can't go back in there. I didn't try
to kill her, but only hurt her because she hurt me. How dare she tell her
kids to disrespect an elder, I know they must be in jail by now; no
home training. You are a product of your upbringing, a child who acts
all nasty and bad, if you go to their home, and then you will see where

they get it from. I've said it before; if they are shown disrespect they will grow up being disrespectful, spitting on people and cussing at them, which is how my friend Lisa taught her children. I went to their home; I knew it was going to be bad. When I walked into the door, the children were cussing and yelling at each other and calling their mother out of her name. I would have put them all out. Men walk out and leave those women unprepared to raise those kids. Boys get big; they need a man around, and the girls need a dad too. They feel like they want to live their lives and to hell with the kids. Some of the kids hit their mom, some have killed them. Everyone saw those things happen, but some people didn't do anything. I remember when I was talking to my friend Sherry, her daughter came into the room and slapped her very hard. Sherry said, "I told you to mind your own business," and they began to fight like two grown women. That girl hit her mom like she was someone in the streets. They fell on the ground and began hitting and biting each other, I told her to stop hitting her mom, but she didn't hear me. They kept fighting from one room to another. Sherry fell and her leg made a loud cracking sound. I looked at her foot and it had stuck between the bedpost and the wall, and it was turned the wrong way. Her foot looked like it was backwards. As she ran after her daughter, her foot got stuck and twisted and broke. She yelled out in pain and I had already called the police and ambulance. When they came to the door, her daughter ran out and down the street. I asked her, "Why would you ever let her hit you, because my children would never hit me." She told me she was fighting her even when she was young, but she could have stopped it before it got to that point. Her daughter's dad told her not to listen to her mom's new husband. He didn't want that man telling his daughter anything. The doctor popped her foot back into place, and she couldn't come back to work for a while, how was she going to pay her bills? That kid didn't care; she just wanted her own way. Sherry said her daughter would not be coming home, but would go to live with her grandma to keep her out of the system. Then I thought she might hit her grandma too. She had other children and I hoped that wouldn't happen again, but they belonged to her husband. I went home and looked at the pictures of my children. They saw a lot of abuse over the years, their father always hitting them, and he would always destroy the little things that we had in our house. They never could go to school with a clear mind, because of constantly being subjected to an unhealthy relationship between their father and I, but they never wanted to hit or cuss me. It bothered me to even be around a child abusing their parent, and I wondered how many parents were getting beat up by their children and suffering from parent abuse. If you raise a child to have morals and values, then they would do unto others what you would have them do unto you. That is a scripture from the bible. I've seen plenty of single parent homes and the children grew up just fine well mannered, and they showed respect to their elders. I have never seen a child act out the way that Sherry's daughter did. At least she wasn't raped; those devilish ways came from her father. He was mad with her mom and then poisoned her against her mom. He told her to disrespect her mom, to hit her and disrespect her own mom and step-dad. I watched and people watched, and some still didn't care if folks watched them, some kids acted out because they were being watched and wanted people to see them act out. I know it's a crazy world. I got sick again shortly after Sherry and her daughters fight and went into the hospital again, I felt my life slipping away from me. They were doing all kinds of test. I began to think they were doing experiments on me and I felt my life slipping away. The nurse came in and told me to take a hand full of pills. I asked what they were for, she said, "I just bring them and you just take them." She said as she was talking to a child. I told her to get me some fresh water, when she brought me some medicine. I put all the pills under my pillow, except the one pill I take for my blood pressure. As the hours went by, I started to feel better. So now I don't want to go back to that hospital, because I don't trust them and when I backed off those pills they were giving me, I began feeling so much better. The side effects were making me sick; I must make a list of all the pills I will not take anymore. I was left in a fearful state of mind. Did they mean to make me sick or better? I kept hearing them say they didn't know what was wrong with me, so why the pills? I found out sometimes it's a guessing game with the doctors. A guessing game I'm not willing to play, that was my life. After a few days of not taking the pills, I was ready to go home and try to pull my life back together. They kept saying the pills were working, but I wouldn't tell them I wasn't taking all the pills. After a few days, they let me out and I had to get food. I ran into James and it had been years since I last saw him. We talked, it was good catching up, but something there wasn't right. I remembered how he had betrayed me and those old feelings came back. I started to cry, I should have just kept walking, because it brought back that pain. I'm in this lonely state of mind now, and I was so afraid to get back into anymore relationships. I'm not sick anymore, but inside I am. As I thought back over my life, I thought some things made me that way, some things I couldn't help and they were not in my hands. In the past, after having strokes, I would remember some things, but I couldn't remember everything and that started to get to me. Did I let people mess me up more? I've been told when you are molested you become promiscuous and follow the path to destruction. I didn't know if that was true, but I did some of the things, and all my friends were broken too, because birds of a feather stick together. I walked around and trusted no one, as I watched people they watched me and everyone's life. Jeana and Mary were dead now; I felt they left too early, only the Lord knows when it's a person's time. I watched other people's children cut up and wondered if my kids would ever treat me like that. I'm feeling a certain kind of way, and it wasn't a good feeling. I wondered what was next? I have had friends and family die and I didn't know how to handle it. I couldn't cry I couldn't feel anything; I was numb to the cares of this life. I know I love my mom and my kids, I have a few friends, but nothing is fulfilling. I try to look forward, but what does forward mean? There are no successful conclusions most of the time. I'm stuck inside this person, and that person is me. All the feelings I feel and no one feels me. What does this mean, now I have been through the bad, the good, the ups and the downs and I can't figure it out yet. When people are not taught being respectful as a learned behavior then you can't hold them accountable for not being able to implement them, goals were not given and they were not learned; they just live day by day. My phone rang, it was one of my friends Ashley and she needed to talk. I went to talk to her, Ashley told me about the problems she was having with her son. He had a runaway while staying in their home. The reason Ashley didn't know was because she hooked up the basement for his bedroom and playroom. He felt like he was in heaven. Ashley didn't have much when she was young, so she wanted him to have everything to make him happy. She had a game room built inside his bedroom; he had his own everything, just like an apartment. His friends all came over to take advantage of his little heaven. They came in and out, even when she was home, she couldn't keep track of who came in and out, she just did everything to make him happy. She worked hard, and then came the layoffs. Then she noticed this young girl name Tamara whom came to her house all the time to see her son. She told her many times, "Tamara it's getting late" and she needed to go home. She would leave and then Ashley's son would sneak her back in the back door. One night she went down there, and they had fallen asleep. She woke her son up; Tamara woke up and started crying. Tamara told Ashley that her uncle raped her and that is why she was there, and then she told her to sleep upstairs with her. She told Tamara, "In the morning we are going to talk to your mom." Well the mom had a different story. The next day Ashley found out that Tamara was giving her mom trouble, more than she could ever believe. After she heard those things, she couldn't believe it. Tamara slapped her mom and stole from her mom; her mom wanted her out of her house. Ashley felt sorry for her, but she heard some of what the girl could do. Her mom said Tamara has a mental problem; she had stolen her mom's car and wrecked it. She did other things like sold items that weren't hers that she took from her mom. The police officers were even looking for her. I felt bad for my friend, and then she remembered that she had started missing things in her house. I told her before don't let Tamara stay one more night there, and she couldn't be trusted. Then soon Tamara ran away. Ashley's son told her the Tamara wasn't anywhere to be found. When her son was asleep, Tamara had taken his keys and made a spare key. She was slowly taking things out of Ashley's house and she was so arrogant about it. I guess she felt that Ashley had more than enough, and she shouldn't care. She couldn't understand those things were not hers, she was crazy as hell. Ashley worked hard to get everything she wanted and needed. She did all that for her son, and she helped to make his life a living hell. That crazy girl started her reign of terror. I found out since she had she had been raped at a young age by her uncle, she hated all men. She started coming in their yard and cutting the tires on the cars. They knew it was her because nothing like that had ever happened before. She was mad because Ashley told her she couldn't live there anymore. She waited until everyone was gone, broke out the windows in the house and left a note, "You won't let me in, so I'll make your life a living hell." Then I felt my life wasn't so bad after everything that I had been through. Then something happened to her Ashley son's car and she left another note, "I can't ride, you can't ride." That car was a gift from his mom and it was destroyed, it was a gift for him going away to college. Truthfully, I don't even know how he finished high school. He had a car to ride back and forth to school, but after she messed his car up, he had to take it to the junkyard. She tore it up and put something in his tank. After the windows were put back into the house, she came by and broke some more out, that time the neighbors caught her, they called a citizen arrest and the police took her to jail. When she got out she wouldn't let up, the police had to be called repeatedly. One day Tamara had some girl bang on his Ashley's door when she wasn't home. She was the most disrespectful young lady; she started to curse and yell that she was there to avenge her Tamara. Ashley's son was home while his mom was at work. He wouldn't let her in then she started trying to break down the door. He called his grandmother, when she got there some big girl was trying to destroy the front door of the house. Tamara wasn't there but she had some friend of hers come and try to break into the house. She claimed she was going to start with the grandmother and beat them all up. Well, I heard the grandmother went into her trunk and that big girl ran, and she ran fast, I could've seen her run, because I would've laughed my ass off. The police were called and said they couldn't do anything until a neighbor came over and told them what they saw. The police located her and chased Tamara until they caught her, and took her back to Ashley's house. They made her tell the truth, and then they took her back to jail. She got out two days later and she was back at their house. Ashley said she was home that time. Tamara started to break a window and she was hit on the head from behind. All the things she did to my friend, she lost it, Ashley said they were fighting. Tamara and her friends didn't realize that Ashley was home this time. Even though Tamara had just turned 18 years old. Ashley beat the hell out of that girl, and another citizen arrest was made as they waited for the police to come and take Tamara to jail again. Then when Tamara got out she came back again and I think this was the third or fourth time. She was up to those same crazy tactics but the neighbors saw her and called the police. The police saw her as they pulled up and Tamara tried to run away, one of the neighbors' kids caught her. The police came and took her to jail again. When she got out again, her reign of terror ended. Crazy thing after that is Ashley's son started seeing this mental girl again behind her back and end up getting her pregnant.

Through all of this she managed to have a baby, she gave birth after all that fighting and going to jail. After she gave birth she slowly started being back to her old tricks. Ashley said people would say that they saw Tamara in the streets all times of night selling something; I guess it was weed or maybe she was selling herself. He told his Ashley he wasn't seeing her, but he wanted to take care of the baby. A blood test was done and it was his child. Tamara made sure he would not have peace in his life. He kept seeing her behind his mother's back. Then he dropped out of school to be with her. He needed to stay in college so he would have a better life. They kept having sex she was his first and she used it. He was silly and nothing his mom told him stuck in his head. She asked him to stop seeing her, but the girl started using that baby. She called him after knowing he had an order of protection against her. He was called by someone who said that they were her step-dad and he told him to come get the baby, she used that baby. He went to get her and about a block away from where the man said he was, that crazy girl jumped out from in front of a bush. She jumped on the hood of his car, she ran on the top and down the back and pretended to fall on the ground. She yelled, "Help me, he hit me." Well she didn't look around good enough; a car coming out of a street saw the whole thing and waited for the police and his Ashley to come. When Ashley got there the witness told what happened, she tried to call him a liar, but the fool ran through a wet yard on a dry day and her footprints were on the hood, roof and back of the car. That time they took her to a mental hospital and kept her there for seven days. Now everyone knew she was crazy, crazy for real. She got out after seven days and went into a homeless shelter. That didn't last long; they kicked her out for fighting with the staff. Then she found a room and called late at night saying someone needed to get the baby, she was put out again and walking the streets late at night with no place to go. Since I was Ashley's' friend, I took her to get her grandchild, but she felt like Tamara would come to her house again to start trouble. I told Ashley that she should take her grandchild to Tamara's mother's house. So, we dropped her grandchild over her mother's. We drove off. Tamara found some place to live and called her mother after two weeks of not even calling to see if the baby was all right. That girl was a real piece of work, when would it end? The neighbors wanted his Ashley to move, their house was the only house the police were at all the time. I couldn't believe the police couldn't hold her longer. She broke the windows three times, cut tires, broke the door, kicked the air filters, stole out of the house, took mail and broke the lights. She did all that property damage and she got out of jail more than four times. Where was the law? They told Tamara if she did anything else that she was going back to jail. Who do you have to go to bed with to get all that, she is so broken? That let me know people can get away with messing up your life, and if you snap and do something, you're the one who gets the short end of the stick. I continued to watch what happened to them and everyone continued to watch me. I went out to dinner and ran into one of my co-workers named Nancy, she came over to my table and started to cry and told me she needed someone to talk to. Her man had just told her he wasn't showing up for dinner, because someone called him and told him that she was no good for him. They told him some of the things they knew she had done in the past, he said it was over and he wasn't coming home. I told her to sit down so we could talk. We both ordered our food and talked about what happened. She met this guy and she wanted to change and settle down. Well, she should have come clean in the beginning and told him she had a past too. Why would he treat her that way as old as they were? He should have known she had a past, I remembered she had that old stalker ex-boyfriend who would mess up all her dates and relationships. But this one was different, she wanted him and he did so many things to make her happy. I said maybe he'll grow up and think about it, he's not an angel. I told her to go home, call him over and talk to him if it doesn't work then walk, he looks better gone. I'm sure he has done some things. As old as we all were, how could someone think none of us had a past? Maybe some had more of a past one than others. People loved to try to mess it up your life and can't seem to mind their own business. A so-called friend told him some things about her, he didn't know if it was true or not, but he is not without sin himself. Then Joel walked up to the table, and my whole mood changed. I told Nancy that I we had to cut this conversation short and I told Nancy that she could call me later if she wanted to. I was so angry. I thought to myself, "Damn Joel just won't stay away, he kept trying to get me back into bed, but it's not going to work. Sure, we have a child together, but I'm not going to have a sexual affair with him. He knew every time I saw him; I gave him the cold shoulder. Joel still showed up at my house uninvited and called all times of the night. I kept saying no, but he thinks someday I will give into him. I said, "I'm having dinner with my friend, go away." He smiled and acted like he didn't hear me. My friend said she was going home to make that call and that she would call me later to tell me what was going on. Soon as she got up and left he sat down until I finished my dinner. He asked, "Can I go home with you?" I said, "Get a life Joel, and get the hell out of my face." Years ago, when I wanted him, he chose to cheat and move a woman into his house. He thought I wouldn't find out, and I'll never trust him again. I finished paying for my dinner and went to my car, and he was still messing with me. I got into my car and drove away to my house. When I got home, Joel was already there, as I got out of my car, he fell to his knees begging me to please take him back. I said, "Have a little dignity for yourself, leave me alone; I don't want you." I opened my door, walked in, and slammed it behind me. At one time Joel and I had sweet passionate love, but that was just me, every time I was with him I felt the after affects. I was so in love I was blind. He was so good to me that was one of my happiest times in life. We traveled and did a lot of things together. He took me to meet his other side of the family. I felt like he loved me, but even they knew that he was a dog. I found out he had seven women, he played them all and I was one of them. He told someone that all seven of his women had some grade A loving and good qualities that he liked. He was just a dog, when I found out I got scared because we had unprotected sex but I was fine, the test came back negative. He was having sex with all of us; sometimes he would have sex with up to three women a day, what kind of man was that? Sometimes I did miss his loving arms and the way he held me and made me feel like I was loved, but he was being fake, we were all just sex to him. I used to cry, but now I can't feel anything. Now I know the truth about Joel and so do you. I got to go to work in the morning; I watched a movie and went to sleep.

CHAPTER TEN – WHAT?

I watched people, and people are crazy; sometimes they don't know themselves. Why do females act like fools when it comes to a man? If he hasn't married you, let's face it, you're just whoring around with him. Some of you ladies want to hurt your man for mistreating you, but the essential point is only what you accept and allow, and that took me a long time to learn. Then some of you don't mind sex with him, that's all they want too. Ladies, he's putting his mouth on you, trying to make you give that up and he's doing that to more than just you. Don't think you're special. If you're in a relationship with a man and it goes on for a long time, it's not going to end up in marriage; it's just a thing that is called sexual friends or fucking partners. If it's good to him and you're the one giving it up and pulling down your panties and spreading your legs, you will let him use you and tell you all kinds of lies. You're not the only one he's sleeping with, wake up and smell the coffee. He's telling you all those sweet lies and whispering in your ear how much he loves being inside of you, it doesn't mean he loves being with you, it means he loves getting it in. I know because a man once told me he loved my pocketbook, and you all know by now what that is. Wake up and stop letting them use you for years with that tired ass lie. I'm not bashing all men. I am just telling the truth from experience. No one wants to be alone, but all of us will be. We all want to be loved, but some people have not been able to grasp the true meaning of what love consists of. When I ask people if they know what love means, every person has a different definition for the word. They say it's a deep feeling, many say its pain, some say it's the giving of one's state of mind, others say its making someone you care for happy, but what is it really? Is it a feeling or state of mind, I don't think they know; I've been told God is love; the purest kind of love and I don't think we understand it. That word love makes some people crazy, then add hate, lust, and control to what they call love. They are willing to fight, curse, do little nasty thing too, and for what they call love! Like keying someone's car, flatten their tires and many other nasty things. If you say you love someone, how could you do anything to hurt them? Even if you break up, you should feel love, so that you wouldn't try to hurt them. That's why I know so many people don't know what love is. These are only my thoughts. After a healing process, I started going out with this new guy name William, he was nice and very good to me. We had a lot of fun together. William was so jealous, every time I would see one of my male friends, he would hit the roof, yelling, and cursing and trying to scare men off. Many men didn't even talk to me when they saw us together. One day he wouldn't answer my calls, so I called James and began talking to him on the phone. We talked for hours and he said he was going to come over to talk a little more, because I was so upset and crying. William called and said we were over. I needed someone to talk to, so I waited for James, and I waited but James never came. Then William called back and said, "Let's talk." I went to dinner with him and we talked. He said he was willing to try it again, he knew he needed to work on his jealous condition. We had a good time together and I did like him. We went back to my house and he was going to spend the night. When I pulled up, there was a car in the yard, OMG, it was James, why was he so late? William asked, "Who is that?" James jumped out and said, "Hi baby, are you all right, I been waiting a little while." William looked at me and yelled, "Are you going with him or me." I said, "He's just my friend." Then he asked, "He's here late, would you let him stay if I wasn't here?" I said, "No, he was here to talk." Then James got into our conversation and he said, "We are good friends, man stop being so jealous she said she wanted you, and I have my life, but we are still friends." William got very mad and told him to leave, James said, "I'm not going until I'm ready, you going to make me?" They were shouting and I said, "Okay James, just go." He got mad and said, "I'm a true friend to you and I have love for you and you're telling me to go, okay, but I'll be seeing you again." William said, "No you won't." James yelled, "Yes I will," and drove off. We went into the house; I just looked at William and shook my head. I said, "I know who I'm with and who I want to be with." James came back yelling at my window, "Are you all right, he better not put his hands on you." I yelled out the window, "Just fuel the fire, just go; you're trying to be funny now and I'm not laughing." I got mad at him because he had a life, like he said, and I felt like he was just pissing William off as a joke. I said one day I'm going to see him and get him back for talking too much and making things worse. I know it looked like I was seeing them both. I did call James over, but William said we were over, so I called James. William didn't want to hear that, he was mad, took a shower and got in the bed; we had to work in the morning. As time went by he wanted to argue, then we broke it off and I'm alone again. On them hot nights I would ride until I got sleepy, go home, and go to bed. While I was driving, I saw a females' butt in the air and her head in the window talking to a guy inside his car, and I saw it was James. I got closer and said, "Hi James, how are you and the family?" He looked around the girl and I knew she wasn't his wife. He looked at me and said, "Hi Auntie, how are you doing, the family is fine." I said,

"So now I'm your Auntie, seems to me I can't be your Auntie, because we should not have done what we did," and I began to twist and wind my hips…mmm, "and it was good too." I said, "Now I'm your Auntie because you trying to make that pickup." James eyes got bigger than they were, he shook his head and the lady walked away. I said, "She looked like a trick anyway." He got mad and asked, "Baby why you did that?" I said, "Remember what you did that night when I was with William, well pay back is a Bitch." While James and I were talking along came my male friend Rene, and he pulled up beside my car. Rene always had a crush and me and I knew it. He was tall, dark, handsome and French. He said, "Hey baby, meet me at the mall in about an hour?" and I said "Okay." James just drove away fast; I didn't care if he was mad. I went home and changed my clothes and went to the mall. He was sitting in his new ride, looking, and smelling good. I said something is about to happen and it's going to be good. We went shopping and had so much fun, here I go again. His accent turned me on and he knew how to treat a woman. He brought me some nice things and he didn't mind spending his money on me. All the haters at work were jealous because they saw how good my man was treating me. I mean he had me looking good. I dressed up daily and went into work; everyone could tell that something was different. When lunch time came, he would take me to lunch. We had many dinners together, and every time he saw me, he didn't want to have sex; or so it seemed. He always gave me a lot of money, maybe that's the way they treat their ladies overseas. That man was so good to me, I felt like I was in a fairy tale and I loved every bit of it. He made my whole house look better. He was so kind and so loving; I had to pinch myself because I wondered if it was true. Everything was going great until someone called me and said that he was sent to me, as some sick joke to see if I would fall for him; and I did. I fell for him, who wouldn't as nice as he was. He was paid to do this by a man I said I would never let him touch me again. They were grown men playing games. He wanted to hurt me bad and that was his way. He had money too, but that's not the reason I fell for him. So, someone paid this Rene to play with my mind and emotions? I thought to myself. I felt something wasn't right from the beginning, but I chose to ignore it; I was hoping people doing evil things to me was over, yet it kept showing up. I didn't love him, but I did care for him. He had me from the start; he didn't have to do that. I called him up and said I needed to talk to him. He told me the truth and said he couldn't do that anymore, and I screamed, "Why me, how could you play games with people lives?" He said he began to feel for me, but I didn't believe him anymore. Here I am alone again. I couldn't understand what they held over his that he would play games with my heart, I told him he wouldn't ever trick me like that again. I was so pissed off. I wanted to go over to his house and bang him on the head with something, but what good would that do? I started to put all the things he bought me altogether, and throw them in his face, but I caught myself and thought, I'm going to keep them and he still can't have me. I hadn't seen his French behind in a long time before now, I thought maybe he went back home to France. Then he comes back to do this to me? I thought something like that supposed to happened when you're young; I didn't know older men played games until then. Will there ever be an end to this dumb stuff; will they ever leave me and my family alone? I started sleeping with my gun nearby. I watched everywhere I went, borderline crazy. One day I said, "That's it, I will not be scared, I will do what I have to do to protect myself and my life." I packed my bags and went down south to visit my friend and get away from the city and all the stuff that was going on. It was so hot, I was having all kinds of fun and it made me not want to go back home, but my family was there. After a week of fun, I headed back. I wondered what new mess would be waiting for me this time. I didn't tell many folks I was leaving, and my mailbox was full. I needed that little vacation so I could come back rejuvenated, and it was going to be easier, because I was on guard. I went to the store and a lady walked in front of me in line, I started to cuss her out, but I held my tongue. No one was going to piss me off right now, I just got back and I still felt good; the trip made me feel relaxed. I was still in that high state of mind and I wouldn't let her take my joy away. No matter where you are in this world, there's a chance that you might get some verbal abuse from some asshole who just wants to test your patience. I left the store and some lady pulled in front of me, I felt like she needed some directions.

Then she said, "I worked hard all my life and I could never get myself a new car like that, why are you having good luck and I'm not, why are some people blessed with fortune and others get nothing, I hate you." She hated me, but I had to work hard to get everything I have, and jealous people have torn a lot of my belongings up, you look at this and think it has been easy? There are people who think they should give up who they are for a person, and jealous people are the worse. Because we allow ourselves to be used, then you want to bust the windows out his car, like the song says. Tear up anything he has, but he will get it all back because a lot of you ladies will buy it for him. I had a man named Terry, for years told me lies, and then one day he told me the truth, which I already knew, but I didn't want to believe. One moment he looked like sunlight, and then he became the blackness I was attached too. He only wanted my body, I pleased him and that's all he wanted, nothing else, no future, no children, no home. That was the last time he even got to smell my perfume that he brought for me. You're going to tell me that I'm just a friend with benefits and think I'm going to continue to let him touch me. We were going nowhere and I had to let it go. It didn't matter to him; he would just get someone who would give it to him. Then he began to mess with my life, telling me I'm not going to just cut him off like a piece of meat. I still belong to him, because I'm older and heavier; who else would want me? There's no one who would treat me like he did. He made me feel like this for many years, then we almost ended up throwing blows. I was ready to fight him. That incident made me think about Joel, but I would soon get rid of him. I saw a friend of mine named John. He was a very big man and I asked him to hang around just so I could get rid of Terry. Terry didn't want any parts of big John, so he soon got the message. John don't play, he looked mean, but he wasn't mean though; but he looked like he was and no one would mess with him. I had the phone hang ups, the doorbell rang and no one was there, until John came around. But I am not any better than him for trying to use someone for my own purpose? I will keep it on a friendship basis. I was not trying to use him, I felt bad when I looked at how I was using him, and oh I know some men who were going through some things too. John had a girlfriend and she treated him like dirt. He loved her dirty underwear; he catered to her and gave her everything she wanted. She dogged him out, and had sex with every man who looked at her from the corner of his eye. He once told me he would climb over me to be with her. I said, "Climb on." One day she moved him in, only because he was a good working man. He bought her a house full of furniture, and she laughed at him and told everyone he was a fool. She was taking all his money. One day he came home early, he said he walked in and he heard someone love making in his bedroom. Then he saw her and some man having sex on the new bed he had just put into the house. He yelled, cried, and walked out. The words he said to me he would have to eat them, he climbed into that. He asked me what he should do, I told him I didn't know, and I had

my own set of problems and I showed the gesture of wiping dust off
my shoulders. After that I was done with using John. I remember one
day I was asked this question, what is a good mother or who was a
good mother? Well she will get up early in the morning to care for her
household, she will give her children what they need to go out into the
world so they could survive. All the worlds' idiots she cries for and
with them, when a heart is broken; she says it's going to be all right.
She'll kiss you when you fall, and hold you oh so tight. You see that
cannot happen when you are just a girl, the cradle rockers of this world
must tell you, with years of hard knocks and eyes full of something
old. She will stick by you when it's hot or cold, that is a good mother.
You could do all those things, but you can't make people do what they
don't want to do. I remember one night my friends and I met this
woman at the club and she looked like she was lost. We always went
out in groups, because we all had haters. She said her name was
Megan and we let her sit down at our VIP seats. They knew us in the
club and we always came together and it was a lot of us. We would set
the whole corner up with drinks, so she came, sat with us, partied with
us. She did what we did; she danced on the table and sang. We just had
a good time and afterwards we would go out for breakfast together.
Sometimes people would wonder why so many women would hang
out together; well we all had been hurt and just formed a thing. No one
in our crew was a lesbian like some of the rumors that we heard, we
were just lonely. We just didn't have a man at that time and were

going through a dry spell, so we started hanging out with each other. Megan started coming with us everywhere we would go. She had a good job, and a beautiful home. She talked about things that made her mad and she had haters too. She had two children and baby mama drama. She said her husbands' girlfriend jumped out of a car and began to hit her; the fight was on the six o'clock news, all in the middle of downtown. I said, "Yes, I saw that on the news, I could tell you needed some friends." Well slowly invited her to our houses and parties. She knew our children and became friends with all of us. Yet there was a side of Megan we had not seen yet. We found out she was a back stabber. She would smile in our face and talk about us to the next person. One day we were all at my house having a picnic, and I heard a yelling match in the yard. I walked out and Megan was yelling at Lee Lee. Well I had to stop it, because she was going to start hitting her and the children were crying. I told them to come in the house and let's work it out. We told the children to play and everything was going to be all right. We went into the house and Lee Lee began to tell me that Megan told someone she knew outside of our group things about us. Her ex-man told her some things about us. I looked at her and said, "I know that is not true, because we don't tell anyone things about each other to anyone outside of our circle." Megan told someone we were all whores and we slept with several men. It isn't anyone's business if they chose to live that type of life, but we didn't want someone around us gossiping and saying things about us. We already had so much hurt in our lives and that was going to keep going on. I told Megan, "You need to get your kids and leave, because we can't do this." So, she got her children and left. You know some of the ladies wanted to kick her on the head, but I tried to calm the anger; our children were still there. We walked down the same road for a while, we had fun; but now it was time to part of our ways. We all agreed to change everything we did, we didn't want to go to the same places and do the same things we were doing, because she would show up. I couldn't stop those ladies from fighting or hitting her. As we talked, she had backbitten everyone and told something about every one of us to someone else. The anger grew, and that's why there had to be a change. The picnic was over they all went home. I was pissed off with Megan. Those women went through enough and didn't need anyone talking about them and causing more pain. We were all trying to work on our lives, and she needed to get one. My phone rang, it was Joel, and he just won't give up. I said, "What do you want?" He said he needed someone to talk too; he was lonely and just didn't know what to do. I asked, "Don't you have someone living with you?" He said, "It's not you and there is no love there." I said, "Humm, you did Joel, you don't know how to love, the thrill was gone, now you want her out, and she wouldn't leave, she has moved in half her family." He felt like it wasn't his home anymore; he said he moved into his own bedroom. They're not sleeping together or they weren't having anything to do with one another. They just paid bills in the house together. I said, "Well what have I got to do with it, Joel I can't help you." I listened to his story and I said, "I got to go" and I hung up the phone on him. Who was I Ann Landers? He hurt me, but now he's hurt, what am I going to do for him? Time to go to sleep; I had to go to work tomorrow. I went to sleep and I began dreaming, I didn't know until I woke up. I was in the arms of a man that loved me, and we were in a loving embrace, the whole world around me was good. The way he loved me, kissed me, and gave me what I came there for, then my alarm clock rang and I woke up. I was so mad, it was so real and it felt so good, but it was a dream. As I awaken I realized my reality. People watch me every day going through the motions, wondering how I have been doing it for so long, and still manage to do the things I do. I have had so many wrong things done to me, I wondered myself. I kept saying to myself things are going to get better, I will find someone like that or he will find me, but it wasn't happening. Is this the way my life will end? Will I be by myself the rest of my life? I thought to myself. I watch people and I see them live and laugh and be happy, why isn't that happening to me? I can't even cry anymore, so numb, so numb. People come over to see me and I don't feel anything, when they talk, I have nothing to talk about, no one shows me love and I don't have anyone to love. They say you create your own happiness. I have tried that, but end up without it; only more pain. I keep thinking how people told me to hold on and be strong, and everything was going to be all right, that can't mean everyone. I wanted to brighten up my life, so I called the ladies and said, "Let's have a party." They all came up with things to do at the party. We called everyone we knew and told them this weekend, we are going to party. We all brought what we wanted to the party, and it was on. I put on my red gown, everyone was dressed formal, and we all looked so good. I took so many pictures and we hired a DJ. That was the party to end all parties. We danced and I had so much fun. Then I began to drink, that always made me so sad, and I would end up very emotional and in my feelings. We all would watch each other's back and hoped no one would tear up the place or fight. It turned out all right, we had so much fun right up into the morning; I was happy. Everyone started to clear out and I felt that old loneliness coming back, but then I heard someone say, "Let's have breakfast," it was Joel. I said, "Let's go." We went to get some food at the place we all go to after the club. We ate our food and talked for hours in the car. That day he was just what the doctor ordered, but I still would not have sex with him. He lifted me for that moment, and for that I thanked him. I knew he was someone who watched me, because he always seemed to be there when no one was. "Where do I go from here?" I asked myself. I called my friends days after the party, just to see how they were doing, or maybe because I just felt alone again. I thought I've gotten over this, but then it creeps back on me. I'm inside my own head and I've been told by Joel that it's bad. He goes to the AA meetings and sometimes asks me to go with him, but I said, "I don't have a drinking problem, I have a thinking problem, and no twelve-step program would help me." Nothing could erase the hate that was shown to me. The next day came and it was back to the grind. I liked the job a lot; I didn't like some of my co-workers though. I didn't care for them because they were nasty; always doing things to get a reaction out of me or anyone they felt were weak. In the past I, would have a lot of outbursts, but as time went on, I saw that's what they wanted to see me do, so I handled it differently. It's a sick thing to do, laugh at someone else's pain, but some people live off others pain. That same year we were having the worst winter that we had ever seen in our lives There was so much snow and it was so cold all of us wanted to leave town, but there weren't too many places in the United States to move where there wasn't any snow. That was the time you wanted to cuddle up with someone special. When it's cold outside, a warm fire, and a little wine to warm you a little more. I thought about all the people I've met in my lifetime and some are not here anymore, what does all this mean? I used to be bitter, but now I feel sorrow. Some people never learn and will never know what's right or will reject it. Out of all the people I know, we think we are smart; but really, we are not. We will never know the true mysteries of this life. Shall we say God is in control or are we getting in his way? The bad things that were done to me from the time I was a little girl, haunted me and made me who I am today. This is a poem I wrote when I was feeling low: I have loved and I have been loved, I have cried and I have been happy. I've been sad, there have been good times and sometimes bad, but I would still thank God for all that I had. I know that he is over watching me, oh so true, and rest assured that he is watching you. After having the strokes and remembering things that made me cry, I have been mad, but I know that I cannot change the past. Can I say that I would have been different, or just confused? There was this fear that I shall be alone the rest of my life, because of circumstances. This is not a book about God; it's about me and the things that happened around me and to me. There are some things I left out, because it would hurt someone dearly. It's still so weird to walk into a room and feel people looking at me, and wondering if they are talking about me. Some people wouldn't have made it, they would have ended it all a long time ago, but I still pressed on. I loved this life for whatever its worth. I watched the news and saw so much murder and mayhem. I was still getting phone calls in the middle of the night. Sometimes people can be an ass; they think they're supposed to say whatever they want to you and you're supposed to take it. I have had it up to here with those kinds of people, how dare they hurt someone's feelings and don't say they're sorry. I bit my tongue today because I was in church, this woman had a cold heart and that didn't belong in the church. If we are not going to do what the bible says, being not liked by many folks is not doing anyone any good. How can you say you are a follower of God's word and hurt someone's feelings? God is love and tells us we should love our neighbors like ourselves. If that's how she loves, I don't want to see her hate. My poor baby was crying because of her, and she never felt that she did anything wrong, heaven is not going to be like that. Grown people sometimes think that they can say what they want, and it's all good, but it's not. They must show respect to get it. People remember what you do more than what you say. Everyone watches you; I'll give you a test, just walk around in your yard, look around and see how many around you notice you and what you are doing. Before you weren't looking, but look hard, now see what you see, sometimes it is good and sometimes it's just being nosey because someone is watching. I had a woman tell me she was my neighbor and I didn't know her. She said she knew when people came and left my house, why was she watching? Didn't she have a life of her own? Now I talk to her when I see her, everyone needs a good neighbor. She didn't come to my house asking for sugar, but she gave me some things, because I had children she was always willing to help me out. The way the world was going, you may need someone to look out for you, but others will watch you for the wrong reasons. Because of people like her, our street was a better place to live. So many things were going wrong, and she was not afraid to say it was wrong and she did something about it, because if the people on this street let everything go on; it would go on forever. I was sitting on my porch and a gang of females came running down the street. I couldn't tell who was fighting who and they didn't care that small children were playing outside. Before we knew it, they were in the middle of the street in a big fight. Grown women throwing blows and bottles, hitting each other with anything they could get their hands on. Mothers were trying to get their own kids out of the middle of the fight. Sister girl got on a bullhorn and everything stopped for a moment. Everything stopped so the babies could get to their parents; they got the children out of the yards and into the houses. Then the police came and beat everyone that began to move. Some of those ladies were mothers themselves, and should have felt some shame, but they didn't. I couldn't tell you why the fight started, just some petty reason. A few weeks later my children and their cousins were watching a movie and there had to be ten children in that room. We heard a pop, pop and I yelled to the children, "Hit the floor," and they were all so scared. Someone shot right next to the house, as I peeked out the window; some guys were shooting at another guy. He was shooting back as he ran down our street. I got on the phone to call the police and the kids yelled, "Don't call, because we may all be killed if the police officers show up at this house." Well, for a minute I thought about what the kids said, and then suddenly, the street was full of police, the kids were still on the floor. I looked out of the window and saw a neighbor next door come out to check out the bullet holes in his car. My heart was in my shoes. The police began asking everyone what happened; you see they have a tracker that tells them when guns are fired. The harassment started when the police started telling folks they all must know who was shooting. When they got to my house, the children were scared. The police officers were so rude when they were questioning the people in the neighborhood; they caused good law abiding citizens to become very mad. We didn't do anything, but we were grilled like we committed a crime; we were born poor, is that a crime? Everybody in the hood is not guilty of crimes. I did all I could do to calm down the children and told their parents to take them home. The mayor of our street didn't know what was going on, and didn't know them; they were all hooded, that's all she knew. People wondered why when folks got a chance they moved away from this neighborhood. There was too much crime, but the rest of us were stuck. Thank God, we have season changes, because when it gets cold, this street turns into dead land. We hardly see each other and it's like the world has taken a rest from the winter stormy weather. I got a call, Rosa's husband got sick and died, she asked me to sing at his funeral. I didn't like him, but I did it. He didn't have any family left, just her and their son. Looking back on our premise lives, make me wonder about how it has shaped us. Now all of us left are still alone, we told ourselves it was over and we didn't think a relationship will ever find us. It's sad to me, things in this book are only some of the things that happened, and people still watch to see. It's true that there is no more hanky-panky going on, well maybe a little, but life is slow now and we are a lot older. It is very important that your children know that you love them. That's something they can hold on to when life gets cold and old things come back at them, trying to bring them down. You see many of us didn't feel loved, and that made us act like the way that we did. My mom loved me, but she didn't tell me some things I needed to know as I grew up, and that left me green. Your children will be green too if you don't tell them things they need to live by. They don't know, help them find it out, so people won't trap them and mess them up in their minds. They could turn out living a deficient life, so tell them everything you know, and tell them to learn everything that they haven't been exposed to as well. As I look back over my life, I see all kinds of things. Some things I wished I could change, like who was my husband, because he was never there for me like I needed him. He was on his own wave length, and he wasn't going to even try anything I liked. He wasn't taught that, or didn't listen. The type of man I needed would have cared about how I felt, and not just himself. My husband was a take it, or leaves it kind of man, I've been told they are all like that, but I don't believe it. There must be someone out there, someone with sensitivity, caring, and someone loving who loves you for real. Someone to wake up too smiling as you sleep, loving you like he does himself. To me right now, it's a lie, I've been looking, but he hasn't come my way. I've just convinced myself to prepare to die alone, without that physical kind of love. I feel pain because my children may have been feeling that way too, because they saw what I had been through, but I hope they find love, I pray they do. Now I think about just how much fun it would have been to have all my grands come over, me and grandpa enjoying them as they played, but our home was broken and they didn't have it. I felt like I failed, because I wasn't carful enough to find out just the kind of man I needed and wanted. Not having a strong and loving man in my life left me out there to fight for myself, and the children and I never liked it. If I would have had a strong man, things I believe would have made me a happier woman. He would have been my protector, my mouth piece; I would not have had to fight alone. I've seen marriages like that; a woman could count on that man for everything she needed. Whenever something came up, he was always there for her and the children. Taking care of all the bills, guiding his family through life, but I've only seen that on TV. Isn't it a shame, I've never seen a married couple act like that. What do I tell my children and grands, to hope that they do find that storybook kind of love? That's what I felt like it was a storybook. My husband sometimes came by to talk to me, I'm polite and sometimes I got angry, because things never worked for us. I was too blind to see it, too young and I was not taught. I felt like I was paying for this in my older years, tired, alone, and sad. Sure, I have some happy times, but being alone isn't a joke. On one of them cold nights or when you feel like you want to cry, and there is no one to hold you. I know that God always watches us, but he can't hold me in the human sense, only spiritually. I know if I had the right man, I would not have been so promiscuous; he would have been my overall. Rosa was having pains too; she was in love with a user, a crack head and he just used her up. He got into some trouble and ran off to Florida and she was down there by his side. She was pining away for him. I told her she had always been so needy. How could she love someone who would continue to hurt and use her? Spending all her money didn't mean a thing. She wanted to have a life with someone that didn't love her; she didn't want to be alone like me, yet she was. She didn't have the money to go back, but as soon as she did, she would, no matter what anyone said she would seek him out. He would use her right now if she had some money left. She went down there with a large amount of money, and sent for him; he went there on a plane. She would let him spend her money; and she was living from paycheck to paycheck and barely making ends meet. He was celebrating with someone else spending her money and getting high with her. He stole some things and he had a warrant out for his arrest, so he came back up here from Florida to do it all over again with some fool. Rosa said as soon as she could, she's going to move back and find her love. "Again," I said, "What love, he is a crack head, he only loves that crack." She acted like she would even leave her son to be with that man. She said when she gets some money; she's going back no matter what. I've never loved a man like that. I look back over my life, and if I did ever love before, it sure is gone; now I'm just numb. All I see around me is crap. I got rid of a man because he wanted to use drugs. I never wanted any drugs around my children, because I didn't want to raise more crack heads and drug attics, I just wasn't made that way. I've had family parties, but never a whole lot of mess going on around. I never had men running in and out of my house because I had kids, and I didn't want them to think that having numerous partners was a way of life. Children are very impressionable, and I didn't want to give them the wrong idea. When I was hosting novelty parties I made sure to have my children stay the night at their babysitter's house. I was always afraid that the same things that happened to me would also happen to them, and I wouldn't be able to forgive myself if it did; my sister would keep them. To be molested makes you scared to do a lot of things, always looking around for something wrong to happen. I've made some new friends now and I see the difference. The folks I hang around now are more stable in their lives, but I wasn't, I didn't know if I ever could be. I'm always watching and feeling watched, from the time I was a child until now; this amounts up to a pile of mess. I wrote this to help me, so you won't make the mistakes that I have made. Being raped wasn't my fault, but a lot of the other things that had happened to me in my past were things that I played a part in. If I had gone the other way, my life would have been different. That Joel is always around, but never wanted to commit. I won't go that far with him, I hold onto that thing they call my heart. I did do some things I loved to do, I sang and I did it well. I used to sing at parties and some clubs; that made me happy. I remember that time I was in a group, and they let me walk down those long flowing stairs, I felt like a queen, I would always receive a standing novation and it made me feel so good. I would always sing my own songs that I wrote myself. Sometimes I would get so mad at my husband because he didn't understand my songs. He doesn't like men coming up to me or talking to me, my singing just pissed him off. I stopped doing everything that I enjoyed doing, and then it just became my will to live and make it for my children. Now they're all grown up and so where do I go from here? I kept in touch with my old friends, the ones that were still living. I called my friend Helen, and she was very mad after all the years we worked for that company, they were not paying her for all the headaches we had working for them. We were forced to live of minimum wage, basically penny pinching and we worked hard every day. We could work overtime to make just a little more, but only once a month and that's it. It wouldn't have been so bad if it was a lot of money, but it wasn't, and then we had to learn all over again how to live. That was the time when I hated the fact no one told me to stay in school. Through all the bad things that happened to me, the least thing I could do was tell my children. Helen had a rough time herself, being abused as a child and sexually molested. She told me she would have sex anyplace and at any time. We were at work and everyone was looking for her, and no one could find her. She slipped away with one man and they used a vehicle to have sex, and they fell asleep. They sent us to find them. I was the one who found them, but I didn't tell that they were in the same place at the same time. She knew she was going to lose her job, so she came up with a story about feeling sick. She knew they were short and she didn't want to go home. She was trying to play it off; our supervisor was a little soft on her, because she did a lot of overtime and worked when she asked her too. She got off a little, she told her next time don't feel so obligated to the job and if she was sick to call off, which she rarely did. She came out of that office smiling. I said, "You better tread lightly now before you lose your job, you need to take care of your children, and that man is not worth it. If he was, he would have taken you to a room after work." I would watch people on that job, there was sex everywhere, and lunchtime was a chaotic situation. They would find empty offices and get it on. I would see it happening all around me but I wasn't looking for it. They were everywhere, in vehicles, in dark corners and in the restrooms. Their spouses probably thought they were all true, but we all knew better. Whenever we had the family days, I would hear some of them say, "He's just a workaholic or all she does is work." They would all put on the show when their wives, or husbands and children were there. I did have my share of fun, but I tried to wait until I got home or went someplace else. Maybe that's the reason someone had been trying to mess my life up, I knew too much. I was watching them and they were watching me. Maybe those sex addicts felt I would write a tell all book. We were all in the same boat. My life was not a sex free zone; maybe I was looking for love in all the wrong places, and I just didn't find it. There were times when I started feeling low, and then here comes Joel again. I wish he wanted a relationship with me, but all he wanted was one thing. That made me so angry, but with him, it's always the same thing. He builds me up and if I give in again, I'm just left with that same old feeling. We could have had a beautiful time together, and then after sex, it's all over, he walks out until next time. I wanted to be with him, because he made me so happy and we shared a lot of time together. He would always tell me that he had feelings for me and it wasn't all just about the sex, but I couldn't tell. For some reason; no matter what I did, I couldn't stop caring for him; this has been an uphill fight. I tried not to love him, but I couldn't run away from him, but I felt like he didn't love me back. I always told Rosa and my other friends to leave their men alone, but I couldn't leave Joel alone, shame on me. How could I give anyone advise about their relationship, and I couldn't get my own love life in order? Every time Joel touched me, I tried to resist, but deep inside I wanted him, so I just let go. I wrote this to Joel: *Dear Joel, you are always in my heart, no matter what I do I can't get over you. I can't lie to my heart anymore. I've told you to stay away from me and sometimes I won't let you inside my house, because you're inside of my heart. I can't say no once you touch me. I have tried to move on, but you keep coming back to mess my head up. You are my love, my friend, and the father of my child. I don't know where we can go from here, but I'm going to leave this town and not come back, because things are not ever going to work for us. No matter how much I love you, I can't make you love me, goodbye.* Then I just tore it up, I'm not going out like that, let him know how I feel so he can just use that against me. He didn't need to know how I felt anyway, I'm messing myself up. Out of all the men I've been with, he touched me the most. Someone started ringing my doorbell and ran away, those people won't let up, and they are trying me. Some man came to my door and told me I better open the door up. He wanted to check my gas meter. I told him to come back with the police and he never showed up again. Someone had my phone number and was calling me all hours of the night. I think I'll change it again, they tried to scare me, but I was about to shoot someone, and I only hope it would be the right one. I saw that it would never end, someone would always mess with me, and if not me, then someone who was weak and didn't have the courage to just run up on them. Thinking back on the past, there has been so much abuse in one family, four generations of molesting going on. Was this some taboo, they just didn't talk about? I got mad when I thought about how they wanted you to just sweep it under the rug, like it was all good to you. One day a little innocent girl was just robbed from under her clothes. She was left with someone she felt was her dad. She loved him, and he was supposed to love her, instead he took advantage of her. He forced himself on her, hurting her and raping her. He told her not to tell anyone, but after he kept doing it, she found out she was pregnant with a child. Then everyone hated her and called her all kinds of names. She told them who did it, but they didn't believe it. When it was told to her mom, he beat them and told them they will let him have his way. Months went by, the child was born, and they acted like everything was good, but it wasn't. She no longer wanted him to get away with this. She took the child and ran. At first, she hated the child and wouldn't have anything to do with it, and then she said to herself, "If I leave her, he will do the same to her." So, she ran with the child. She had grown to love her baby, and she wouldn't give him a chance to put her in harm's way. He wasn't going to touch or violate her baby the way he did my mother and me. Many people don't want to share their story of what happened to them. Some get rebellious, some crazy, but we need to do something about it, not just sweep it under the rug. Little girls' minds are being manipulated, and when their abusers tell them to never tell anybody, the little girls keep it a secret because the abuser makes them feel dirty, and they think that people would frown on them and their actions. In actual reality; the girls do not have the ability to distinguish the difference between making love to someone, and being raped by someone. The abuser always makes sure to go over the one ground rule, which was to never tell anyone what they do because people would think they were dirty, and nasty. The girls would let the abuser affect their minds, there thoughts, and spirit would be twisted up and warped into believing love was supposed to feel that way. Eventually they would adopt the philosophy that they have no say in what their abusers do to their bodies, and this was because society has a way of deflecting these types of issues, and try to force people into adopting the philosophy of being taboo. Some of them can't live with the shame; it puts them on a path of self-destruction. After she got away from him, she turned her life around, and she strived to give her daughter a better life. Her mother met a man, whom she didn't trust, and she would always wonder if he would do it to her child and it turns out he did. She wasn't going to live like her mom, and she left because her life was full of abuse too. Then her husband was killed and she felt a weight was off her shoulders. Not that she was glad he was killed, but glad that she didn't have to go through the fights and the beatings anymore. Time went by and her little girl became a woman, and she had a little girl. She trusted her own dad to keep her safe, but he raped her little girl. He got inebriated one day and molested his own daughter. Tears fell down my eyes as she told me that, how could this happen to the same family so many times? This has happened for so many years and numerous amounts of time but people won't talk about. As I watched her get older, I knew something was wrong, but I dare not ask, because I would have to tell what happened to me. It gets painful when I think back on it and all the anger comes back to me. I think about my abuser even though he is now dead, he asked me on his death bed to forgive him. He called for me as he was dying, and told everyone to leave the room except me. I was so afraid, he cried out for me to forgive him. I yelled, "No, do you know what you have done to me, my life was a living hell because of you, I could never forgive you, no, no, no." That's when my mom found out. She cried and yelled, "Why didn't you tell me?" I cried, "I didn't want to hurt you, I felt I could keep it to myself and you would be safe, but then you put him out and I tried to live it down." But I still can't Lord; I still can't live it down. It makes it easier because he died, but it's not gone, because I will always have to live with this. So much mistrust in my heart. I cried as he hurt me, and he showed no mercy, and I didn't have any at that time. Now I think I must forgive so I can go on from here. Hearing her tell me of the hurt and the shame she went through, brought back the pain and the shame I felt. She said after her molester died, she began to live. This book is not a tell all, it is a release from pain, how I and others were used and taken advantage of, misused, stalked and made a fool of. In my mind, I need to find a way to get over what I can. I grew up around so much fighting, it was nothing to us in the neighborhood to see ladies being beat up, children being abused and parties even happened. Never peace, we were not taught about peace and quiet, love and respect. Some of us did learn it as we got older, but some didn't, they missed the boat and their poor children suffered more. People sometimes are amazing, they do all kind of things that mess with other folks, why not just let someone live their life like they want to live. Why try to do God's work for him, do they not know that he is watching just like they are watching. For every wrong turn, they thought that they got away with. They didn't fear God, and they thought he wouldn't do anything to them. But you reap what you sow, and it will come back to you. Maybe the folks you hurt might not see it, but you will reap it. I felt like I had been pulled into so much chaos and yes, I speak my mind; sometimes it might not be what folks like, but I said it. If I see that a teacher is not teaching my children right, I have the right to say something to make it right or take them out of that class. Folks think because you don't say anything all the time, you don't have the right to say something when you need too. May God have mercy on us, because we have left the Father if it has come down to that, and I'm starting to feel a certain way; they say the devil is busy, but it is the people. It's a shame when you feel like you don't belong anymore. I found that people were trying to make me fight those battles. If they didn't like someone, they would try to use me to hurt who they disliked. They'd call me and talk to me and I talked with them, but I didn't trust them. I would never trust people because they are evil. Months after my brother died, many things were going through my mind. His wife wanted him cremated and we wondered why. She wanted to get rid of his body as soon as she could. Were there some drugs in his body that she wanted never to be found? She didn't want to have a funeral for a man she claimed to love so much. Not even wanting his mom to grieve for her child or see him one last time. She was surprised to know that he had been coming down to my house talking about her to me. The months leading up to my brother's death, why she began doing strange things? He began to get so sick, she wasn't around; always working and never around. He was sick all the time. I got a call one day from the hospital, said my brother was dropped off at the emergency department and he was just clinging to life. I got my mom and we went to the hospital. They told us he was brought there just in time, that time he didn't die. He had been given something to eat that wasn't right. When you are poor, doctors don't do a drug screen unless they thought something was wrong. You see, she was a nurse and there were some things she knew that we didn't know; it was like he was slowly dying right before our eyes. She had gone down south for weeks on end, and he didn't hear from her. He came to visit me; he was very sick; to me it looked like his life was slowly being drained away. He had fainted on his job earlier and they sent him to the hospital. They said his blood sugar was 660, and that's what lead him into a Diabetic ketoacidosis, which was a life-threatening condition for diabetics. She was a nurse yet she was never around to take care of her sick husband. Could she have been poisoning him and wanted to be gone the time that he died. This time we talked, I cooked him lunch. He told me she took all his money and he couldn't pay for his truck. I called social security and told them she took his check. They told her that in so many days, that money must be back in the bank in his name. Two days later she sent him $1,500 dollars to save the truck for him. She was to put the money back into his account. Then I asked him what was going on, he wouldn't tell me, he only said, "I'm not really a single man." I said, "What does that mean, tell me." A lot of the family was over, mom too, so we couldn't talk about it. She always said she was working, but she had been seen all over town with another man in a black truck. I remember one day we cleaned his apartment out, we found her check stubs. There wasn't much overtime, in fact, there for a while there wasn't any. So, where was she at? Family picnics and other dinners we had, I couldn't prove it, but something was wrong. I found out she was the one who dropped him off at the emergency department. Some nurse, she had to go to work despite the fact her husband was near death, and she refused to take the night off. Just before the car accident, my brother came by to visit me; he could barely make it up the steps. He had been found again on the floor and near death. She picked him up, washed him off and took him to the hospital. We were told his wife and her kids had gone to Florida. I was waiting for him to call me, I called him but I couldn't get through to his phone, but he was in the hospital. She told him they didn't want to worry anyone, what kind of nurse is she? I know she knew about medicine and knew just what would hurt or harm him. If he had high blood sugar, why was he eating everything under the sun? She had talked to him and told him that he could no longer have sex with her and she needed someone. He told me, he told her to go get someone. The holidays were coming, and we planned for a dinner like we always did, but she didn't show up. He told me with tears in his eyes, that she was in Florida looking for a place to live for them. He was sick; he could hardly make any trip. I said, "Something isn't adding up." She came back for three weeks and put him into his own apartment. She took half of the furniture and put it in his house, and the rest she kept. My sister called her, and she told her my brother and she are over. Yet my brother was telling everyone she was coming to get him when she found a house; who was telling the truth? When we went to his house, it was all set up for him to stay there and not leave. Her clothes were in boxes and he was going to ship them to her. Why not take him with her if she loved him like she said? He told me something was wrong with his car earlier that day. They told me at the hospital that the car accident killed him, by the looks of him; he was on his way out anyway. We rushed up to the hospital to see him after the crash. He was talking out of his head, but he said the gas pedal got stuck and the car took off. There were so many things unanswered surrounding my brother's life and death that we may never know. There were a lot of people who questioned what was going on. That woman had his body burned, and we thought she was covering something up. We found all kinds of sweets in his house, if he was a diabetic, why did she stack up his house with sweet stuff like that? None of his meds were used. Some old voodoo was in that house, and some weird looking white powder, you be the judge. She came back to town to get the rest of his money. Someone went into his apartment and ransacked the place. They took all kinds of stuff, I had absolutely no clue about his assets, but when my mom and I got there, everything was a mess. We cleaned it up and took everything out of his place to the Goodwill store, and that was the end of it; or so we thought. She kept saying she was going to take mom to court, was she bi polar or what? She said she had things in the house, we didn't even know who got the stuff. Then she started watching us, sitting outside my mom's place. She called the police and told them I was going to kill her. I was still upset about my brother and I think she was the cause of him living such a miserable life. I didn't want to do anything but cry, but I couldn't. She wiped out all his bank accounts and didn't even want him to have a decent burial. She said she loved him, she loved his money, because she took it all; she's going to get hers one day. She told my sister she wanted a meeting at my house, but why my house? She was supposed to be my sister in law, but I hardly knew her. All those years' people had been bringing trash to my door and dropping it off. She was trying to swindle us out of money. She told the hospital to tell his family to take care of anything they want to, she had a life in Florida and she wanted nothing to do with it. What kind of love was that, I think was bi-polar? Then she hopped on a plane and she got here to stop all the funeral plans we made for him, that nasty piece of work. My mother cried all night long, and I wanted to kill her. She wanted to take his body to church, but the church said no because of the things she did. Then she made plans and said, "You all are going to pay for it." We were going to give him a nice celebration of life ceremony and she ruined it, until the point that my tear ducts were dry, and I couldn't cry another tear. There was only anger, why did she come back, and she was crazy if she thought she was getting a dime from this family. I did all I could to keep the whole family off her. She got up and ran out shouting, "I have the power, and he will be cremated in the morning if you all don't give me money." My whole family chased her and wanted to kill her, but she got away. She got in her car and drove off yelling out the window ha, ha, ha, just to mess the whole thing up; she was crazier than I figured. We called the funeral home to make the service and she had already told them to burn him up. They told us if we could come up with the money for the service, we could have it. He was a vet and she even tried to get that money. We had the funeral after they burned him up, so whatever she did it's long gone. We went in my brother's house they found pictures of her laying in nasty poses, dirty hoe. His poor son was left with nothing but the pain he felt. All his life his dad didn't love him and this was the clarification he needed to justify him feeling that way because his dad gave her access to all the money he was saving for him. When she married him, she made him change everything. Not wanting to even see his own son, she was always telling my brother he had a new family, and not saying it just to him but all of us. In our family eyes, she was the scum of the earth. She caused so much pain for all of us, why? One day I spoke up for myself, but the people that I thought supported me ended up turning their backs on me for expressing how I felt. Not my close friends, but some other folks I knew. They were supposed to have my back, but they made sure to show me that they didn't. Why is it that women that are messy are always trying to fight and take over, who are they to think that nobody will say anything to them? When I do it, it's thought to be evil on my part; it makes me want to say, "What the blip blip." My friend Anna called me and wanted me to take her to the food mart and I said I would. I got over to her house and her mom was there too. They both wanted to go get food. I helped her mom into the back seat and drove to the store. We walked and talked, and then Anna dropped down to her knees, she had to hold onto me. She had something wrong with her, it was a tumor, and as I tried to help her up in the store. In the past I told her to get that tumor out, well I hadn't seen her for weeks and she said she was okay. I thought she had the surgery, but she had not done it, that's why she was bleeding so badly right now in the food mart. She had on light pants and you could see the blood all over them. Someone called 911, but they were taking too long. They put her on an office chair, she fainted and her eyes rolled back up in her head. Her mom was old and frail and she began to yell, "Help, help, help her." The blood was coming out very fast, she was wetting up the towels the employee was giving me. They were taking too long, I rolled her out to my car, and they didn't want her to die in that store, so they helped me roll her to my car and three people helped me put her in the car. Her life was slipping away and I had to get her immediately to the emergency department, and we put her in the back seat. When I got to the emergency department, they took her out of the car. I told them she had a tumor and it must have burst. They saw the blood and took her to surgery, they didn't waste any time. Surgery took six hours, I couldn't stay and I told her mom to call me when it's over and she did. The next morning before I went to work, I went to see her. The doctor said if I had waited for the ambulance, she would have died. She had lost almost all her blood, she only had one pint left and minutes later she would've been a dead lady. She slept for about three days. I walked in after she woke up. She had the nerve to ask me why I had not been there. I told her what happened and I told her, "I was the one who saved you." I told her I have been there to see her, but she was asleep. They said I saved her life, until this day we are friends, I love her like a sister. Over the years, we were always in each other's life. We sang together and we cried together, we've been through so much at the same time. Even as I got older I still watched people and I still feel them watching me. When I walk into any place, there are eyes on me, is it because we all possess the same type of spirit? There are some folks, that as soon as I walk up on them, I don't like them. I've tried to change this, but it's in my spirit and we didn't click. I've been told that we must love people with the same love God has, but dislike is not love. I met a man, his name was Mann and he was a piece of work. From the day, I met him, he would stare at me, made me feel so out of place. He tried to have me, but there was something not right about him. Well he looked at me like he had never seen a lady before. It felt nasty for some reason, like his eyes were licking me all over. Like I knew he was a sex maniac. He started coming to my door trying to talk to me, telling me all he was going to do for me. I would talk to him through the door; he wasn't getting into my house. Mann always brought me gifts, and then one day he asked me out. My cousin told me something about him, and I felt maybe she knew more than I knew.

I still didn't want him in my house. One day I told him I would go to the movies with him, but I would have to drive; because I had that trust issue thing going on. We went to the movies and it was all right. He told me Mann was his last name so, that's what they called him. I noticed he did a lot of talking and then he started to break down about what happened in his life. Every time I tried to talk, he would tell me to be quiet and let him talk. I felt like he needed to vent, so I listened Then he started to tell me his wife had left him and taken a lot of what he had worked for. He hid some of his things from her years ago, so she didn't get it all. I knew his gifts cost good money, I liked the gifts, but I wasn't going to use him for money, because that's not me. He tried so hard to make himself look good. Everything he did, made me feel liked and wanted, but I couldn't feel anything for him. As time went by, he became very pushy and loud. He started telling me to shut up all the time and that he likes his lady quiet. I wasn't going to yell, cuss and fight with him, so I stopped going places with him. Now I feared him, because he told me he would put his hands-on women. I told him no more dating and to go away. He told me he would take me to the park and give me an attitude adjustment. I said, "What attitude adjustment?" He said that's what he does. He said every time he caught me in the streets, he was going to take me to the park and beat me up, and leave me there like he did his ex-girl. No wonder the poor ladies left, but he got the right one baby. I know the arts and I'll kick him into next week. I said, "Back away from my house now, or I'll kick one of your eyes out and you won't see where you are going, you better go now or you will get a new attitude when I adjust yours." He left and then two days later he yelled up at my window, "Give me back everything I brought you." I started throwing his junk out the window, until I got to the big things. I said, "No more walk away or you're going to get it." I pointed my nine millimeters at him and said bye, bye and he ran to his car. Sometimes a girl must do what a girl should do. I laugh at that now, but it wasn't funny then. I've seen so many folks go through so many things, some good and some bad, people don't change. My friend Sally called me and wanted to vent. Well she listened to what everyone else said at our meetings, but this time she felt it was time and she could no longer keep it to herself. I was around her and I knew she had a story to tell. This lady was verbally abused. They talked about the way she looked; she had red hair and blue eyes, no one else in her family had that. Everyone teased her from the time she could remember. You see, she was a brown skin black girl; her hair was red like a white person. Others in her family talked about her and said, "Where did mom get you from, did you really come out of her?" She would cry and tell her mom. Her mom would only say, "I love you no matter what you look like, you're my child," but that wasn't enough. When she went to school, everyone picked on her because she didn't look like them. She would look at you with those piercing blue eyes, and it did kind of put you on end, it just didn't look natural. We all knew she was of mixed race, but what a combination.

She was a good woman, she took care of her children and loved her husband, but he wanted other things in life, so he left. She had feelings, no matter how she looked to anyone. We all hung together and we didn't talk about it, until she told us how nasty people were to her as she grew up. My heart went out to her as she told her story. Why the color of skin matters, someone tell me, because when you get right to it, we are all people. This is about my brother Thomas. He was very smart and got a very good job when he got out of school. Thomas was watched as he got higher in a well-known company and he had haters. He got the manager's job and the haters would try to sabotage his work. He was called to come in and implement some new adjustments, and that led to letting folks go. It was their own fault, but they blamed him. Thomas was sitting at his desk and someone called him out on the line. He went to see what was wrong, quickly fixed it and went back into his office to finish his coffee. When he took a drink, at first it burned when it went down, maybe it was still hot, they say he finished it. After a few minutes, he let out a yell and they said his insides were burning. He started to foam at the mouth and blood came out too. They called the ambulance they said you could smell chemicals coming out of him. His lips were burned as he was hanging on to his dear life. When they got him to the hospital, they tried to get most of the stuff out of him, but didn't want to make it burn him anymore. We got there and he looked lifeless, the doctor said his brain didn't get enough oxygen, so he was experiencing hypoxia, and if he pulled through he would have brain damage. As the days went by, he started to talk and we knew he was never going to be the same. He began to talk about rainbows in the sky with money falling like rain, or an angel driving down our main street in a jeep, many crazy things. They kept him in the hospital for a while, and then they had to put him into a mental health facility for five years. They said we could've brought him home, but he was like a six-year-old child in his mind and just crazy. He is now in his fifty's and still the same, crazy. People laugh at him and some run, but I still love him. Jealous people made him like that. The company said they would take care of him for the rest of his life, what life, he didn't know what was going on. He laughs and talks to himself, looks up in the sky, points and talks to who knows. They didn't feel anything, but the loss of one job, their life goes on, while he is paying for climbing up the ladder with hard work, now he's just crazy. Everyone in my family should make sure he eats, change his clothes, and stay safe, because he is just a child in his mind. Sometimes I cry for him and always pray for Thomas.

CHAPTER ELEVEN – WHAT IS JEALOUSY

It's when you can't stand someone else having something or doing something that you can't do, and if you can do it, that person can always do it better than you. It's like cancer; it forces some people to do some nasty things, because they can't have you looking better than them. They don't like others having more material things, why? Don't they know they're going to die someday and someone else will get it anyway? People play tricks on each other and tear up each other's stuff. We're all working people, we're not ever going to be rich, so we cause our own people to have to struggle even more. But you still can't get ahead, and you are still stuck in the same environment as everyone else. All the people who were responsible for being devious and caused discontent were dead, well everyone is still in the same neighborhood and no one is doing better than the other. They tried to tear someone's life up, but they were so dumb, they didn't take the time to better themselves. All that time wasted on tearing up others, and it came back to them. Some of the people were dead now, and some were out of work, and all the others were sick. They didn't do anything because we're all going to live until we die. That's a sad way to live, they want what I have, and they want what you have, but they are still poor, and they tried to make me the company of their own misery. You see, what goes around comes around. I eat everyday like them, drive like them and I'm happy. As I look back, it was just a hot mess, and for what? Have you ever walked into a place and your eyes catches someone else's eyes? But you didn't like them. Some of us ladies show hatred for no reason. I always held my own, by that; I mean I never got into a competition with anyone. I got what I got and there was no problem. My sister tried to say that I couldn't get a man because I was thick, seems like men were attracted to this thickness. I was always confident in myself when it came to getting a man, because there was always a man trying to push up on me. I got these big brown eyes and pretty face, I never had a problem. Maybe that's what caused them to hate me, but don't hate me because you can't get it or because I'm beautiful to a man. Then you need to have some good conversation, or was it that I was always ready to give it up. At some point, it made me feel wanted; sometimes I would just look at myself and say, "What got it again?" When you're not told about relationships and that love may take a little time. If you go at something full force, you get it or you don't. Why do some people get mad when it doesn't come their way? Some ladies want a man and he don't want them, and they try to make it happen. If he wants you he will show it, don't try to make him want you, when he doesn't. Don't get mad when he steps to someone else, life is to short; walk on girl, look for something that's meant for you. I watched people make fools out of themselves trying to force someone to be with them, why? There is someone for everyone, but they try to force someone to be with them. We are getting older, and you think things would change, but they don't. My friend Nancy called and asked me to go for a ride with her, and I did. We pulled up to this house and she said, "I'll call him and he will come out." I said "Who?" She said her husband and when she called he came out. She jumped out the car and began yelling and hitting him with a small bat as he was running. I sat there looking at the whole thing; I could not believe my eyes. She had been following him and

215

knew that he was cheating. She hit him until she got sick of it, she got in the car and we went home. She called me on the phone crying, and I felt so bad for her. She never thought he would do that, but he did. Is there anyone out there not cheating? So many families are broken up, because of this; poor children are the ones who suffer. They no longer have two parents at home, only one and that one struggles to take care of them by themselves. So many times; I felt like I was losing my mind, I had to act older and take on adult responsibilities. I saw things in the dark, sometimes I would see children playing and running in the house. I would yell and tell them to stop running in the house, then get up and no one was there. I looked down the hallway and saw a man combing his hair, and when he saw me; he vanished into thin air. So many things were done to me, and it caused this; until I pulled my mind back together. That is what those haters wanted me to do, so I pulled it all together. Some people said go get help, well I felt that would only make it worse and not better. They would only put me on meds and I was already taking plenty of medications for other health issues and conditions. People did crazy things that were hard to understand, but I kept that to myself. All the time they laughed at me, because I couldn't prove how things happened. I would cry sometimes, all alone and I felt no one would help me. I grew up in a ludicrous environment, and I lived a ludicrous life. My life was not a joke to me, but to some it was. That made me do some promiscuous things, I never used drugs, but I had family members that did. Let me tell you, it was a trip; they would say and do anything to get those drugs. They would steal meat and everything. We were having a picnic and we seasoned up the meat and left it on the table. We were in the backyard and the grill was nice and hot. I went back into the kitchen where the meat was, and there was no meat. We had marinated a lot of meat and there was nothing there. My family member took the meat out the front door and sold it for drugs while we were in the backyard. My neighbor saw him go out the front with the box of meat and ran. We were all pissed off and we had to go get some more meat to cook. She also saw him take his new shoes his mom brought him and sold them for dope. I don't trust anyone; so much had been done to me, until I found it hard to trust people. People had been trying to mess my life up for some years now, I question everything people do to me and for me. I always felt they were out to get me. Every time I let my guard down, someone lets me down. While growing up I did trust, but things around me made me back away from some folks. It is the worse feeling when you feel someone has betrayed you. It made me think about my ex name Bradley. I mean he would kiss you so gently and then turn around and stump on your back. It takes a little love out of you, not in a good way, but the worse way. Man, that hurt. It's like was he ever my man or ever a friend? Why did he have to stab me in my back? *Ohhh, that hurt, take that knife out of my back you bastard.* I thought to myself. He would smile in my face and then go talking behind my back, I wondered what else had been done to me. He should have been there for me. The correct way would've been to come to me and do anything to help me; if he was truly my man or my friend. I remembered he had me wait for him to pick me up and he never showed up. My blood was boiling, now I don't trust him. He wanted to use me and thought he was going to walk out on me and not say a word to me. He owed me that much, he knew what I had gone through, was it a joke to you too? Your silence tells me that you are guilty of something or hiding something, because you would have called me. You're just like the rest, and you swore to me you were not like that, your loss, and someone else's gain. I'm used to doing for myself anyway, life goes on. I've been trying to find a man that would be there for me, my soulmate, someone that will be there for me, through the good and the bad. But I think it's not meant for me, I let my guard down again and got the short end of the stick. He told me to act like I don't know him whenever I saw him with his new woman. He never told me about her, and it was a shock to me when I found out. We had been going out to the club and just kicking it, he was another club person. He saw me sitting by myself and came over and began talking to me that night. All my friends were there, but I felt so all alone, so while they danced; I was zoning. He came up and began to talk, I didn't hear him at first, then he touched my arm, I looked up at him and said, "Get lost." He held my hand and asked me to dance, I said, "Get lost." He said, "Now, I'm not the one who made you mad, don't be nasty to me." I just looked at him and felt, well maybe I'm being nasty to someone I didn't know, but those fly by night men at the club only wanted sex. This time I wasn't giving in, but he was gentle and I began to talk. The girls came back after dancing and we kept talking. It was time for the club to end, as I was leaving, he asked me for my number and I gave it to him and went home. I had been feeling lonely and tired of going from man to man. I wanted to find my soulmate, so all this clubbing and breaking up with losers would stop. As I talked with him, I asked if he was married and he said no. I said, "Okay, I need someone just to talk too right now." So, we talked and took long walks, well I just felt that he would be my friend. The ladies laughed at me and said, "Are you in love Miss Thing." I quickly said no, he's just a friend, and I should have kept it that way and I wouldn't be feeling this way now. I began to like him because he seemed like he was always there, but I wasn't going to take it to that next level, that sexual level; no not this time. I felt maybe he was my soulmate, but I would wait and see. He took care of me and didn't act like he was in a hurry to have sex with me. We had so many good times together. One night he asked me out and said, "Are we going to take this to the next level, I really care for you and I'm going to do right by you, for whatever you need and want; but not tonight, we can wait, until we do this, I need it to be right." So, we made plans to go away, it was a nice place, we had dinner and got into the hot tub. Then we went to our room, it was so nice, he took his time and he didn't rush into it. He was so gentle and loving with me, he made love to me, and it didn't feel like it was just sex. Once again, I was sucked in by a man. Months had gone by and we were having a good time, until he called me one day and said he needed some time to think about things, about three days. He said, "Don't call me or try to see me." I felt like he was telling me to get lost. That pain I used to feel came back into my heart, tears filled my eyes. I called in sick the next day, but I did call one of my friends. I was crying so hard, I said, "No, no, not again." She came over, I was sick and I didn't even get dressed. She said, "Call him, maybe he really needed you and was just doing things this way until he gets it right, but maybe he really needs you to call him." So, I did, and a woman answered his phone; I knew I didn't dial the wrong number; I had my baby on speed dial. She said, "May I help you," I said, "Yes may I speak to David." She said, "My husband is not here right now, can I take a message?" My tears stopped and I said, "No I'll call back." I began to boil, my friend Shelby asked what was wrong, when I told her, she began to get mad too. She said, "I can't believe him, all those months and he's married, where was she, you've been to his house, there was no sign of her and was she just coming back to him, he should have told you the truth." I believe happiness was never going to find me. I wasn't willing to look or wait anymore for that real love to find me. For months, I've been alone, I got mad when a man tried to talk to me. I'm through, it's never going to be in my life and I got mad. I don't want my children to live like this, I hope they love, but my life is not what they should follow. I've made it a point not to let them see or know everything I've been through, because they would have no hope like me. I said it's because of what started me on this path. Sometimes I wished I could have been nasty like other people, not saying I'm better, but I watched the way they treated others and I didn't like it and I chose not to be like that. Who or whatever was warning me of things to come, didn't want me to be nasty. But I took more than the normal person should have taken in my life. I have looked at folks who said they were happy, but were they or was it all a lie because what I hoped for didn't exist. Happy couples acting like they're in love forever, no I don't know anyone like that. What I saw was, if the parents are messed up, sometimes the kids are and then some are messed up on their own. I stayed in the house all the time, now I wasn't working and this is what my life had become, me looking out the window wondering, what now? I thought about all the things that went wrong and there was no love, or was there? Joel used to tell me he loved me, but how could that be when he caused me so much pain. He didn't want to marry me and spend the rest of his life with me, he just came around to have sex which was so good that he left me throbbing and he would just disappear. There was always something there that didn't last too long. Then, I remembered my ex, Jess told me he loved me too, but why didn't he leave them drugs alone? All those lies and I didn't trust anyone, and they both made me think this even more. Everything I looked at now was not good for me; the only thing I loved was being a mom. I loved my children dearly and I thank God I have them. I called my friends to talk and nothing had changed for any of them, it was the same old same old. Rosa was still bored and stayed in the house all day long and wouldn't go out. She was a hermit, she wasn't looking for her destiny or anything, just a bump on a log, talk about a turn around. I wish I could live where she lived because I would never be home. I live in cold weather and I stay inside most of the time. All the other ladies were planning a big meeting so we could get back together and remanence about old times. They were trying to get me out of the house, but cold air was not for me. If only Rosa and I could change places, I'll take it. Every day I talked to her, she made me mad, I would be enjoying that life she has, its warm where she is and cold where I am. I thought about this, sometimes God watches everything that happens, what do you think he thinks of it all, did people truly care? As I've said all through this book, people are watching you; they watch what you say and do, what does this all mean? Just when I was feeling low, James contacted me. We had a nice talk and now it doesn't hurt like it used to, but I still have love for him, he still had it. His words were like having him hold me oh so tight, rocking me and taking away all my fears; oh, I needed that. There would never be us, but just thinking about what we once had took my mind back to what it was like. Rosa and I had a talk, and even though I got mad at her for some of the things she had done, I knew that I had also done some awful things as well. She kept saying there was not going to be that love we had been looking for in our lives. The perfect man is not real, not the one she and I have been looking for. Sometimes she acted like she didn't love that dope head she's been pinning over. My mind is numb when it comes to loving a man; I've been hurt too bad. I think if I wasn't molested when I was young, my thoughts would have been different. Someone told me I had to forgive and to forget, it's hard. They said it was better to have loved and lost than to have never loved at all. I wished sometimes I never would have loved, then there would be no pain in my heart when I thought about the love I'd felt for a man. Jess still called me and it seems like dead air, I didn't have anything to say after all the things that happened. He asked how were my children and how have I been, afterwards we sat there quiet until one of us said, well just wanted to see how you were and hung up. Jess thought I was going to call him over to play hide the salami, but I could get that anywhere if I wanted it. I'm older and I wanted something more lasting, I've learned that sex is not love, it's just lust and we all feel that, but acting on it in my ripe old age is not what I'm looking for. I needed some of that sweet loving, that old hug me, kiss me, hold me and rock me kind of love. The kind I thought the old folks had but he was he had much baggage; baby mama drama. He had a crazy girlfriend and a wife that suffered from a sickness, too much for me and we would never be happy. Maybe in bed, but it wasn't worth it. I placed him a little lower than Joel, and that's low. I looked at all that stuff and thought, I'm grown now, because things mean something other than what I felt they used too. This book has freed me in so many ways, I let go of the hate and the pain I once felt, so thank you all for reading my life's story. Look around you and see the life around you will find stories too. I hope you didn't go through as much pain. I think it's time to have a party; mama was turning seventy- nine years old. We all put together the party to end all parties. We all had a very good time; she is getting around good for her age. I try to make her happy; I feel we should, because she had been through so much in her life. We tried so hard to make her life as happy as we could, we loved her so. As the party was going on, I watched the way everyone made her happy, and that made me happy; all older people should be happy. The family was so close and I hope we all are happy. But there is always something getting in the way, for all the good, there is some bad. You can rest assured that old bad stuff will creep back into your life. Everything could be going so good and someone or something messes it up. Some of the ladies I used to hang with are not my friends anymore, if you say you are my friend, why would you betray me? If I say I'm your friend, I will go to the limit for you, and if you do business with someone and they think you are getting anything more than they have, they want to tear you down. They will talk about you and try to get everyone on their side; you're not going to live anything down. You somehow become the lowest and dirtiest in their eyes. This lady told me that the house she was living in had ghosts and acted like I put them there. She said her baby was sick because of the house, he couldn't sleep and she couldn't sleep; she turned out to be a real ding bat. The landlord fixed the heat and she still had the heater cleaned, he did everything to make her happy, except take her to bed. This is what she was mad about now. Then she began finding things wrong about the place. He was my family member of mines and she quickly got mad because he didn't want to make love to her. Then I'm not her friend, because I won't talk him into her bed. If that's why she moved out; then let it be. Now she is just someone I thought I knew I hope she doesn't call me anymore. It's like losing a family member, like a death. As I think back, Rhonda and I became good friends and we didn't start out like that. Mr. Devil sent her to beat me up, she stepped to me, but no one told her I would step back. She walked up on me at the job and began to cuss me out, telling me just how she would kick a bone out of me. I stood their toe to toe, eye to eye; waiting for her to try it. My brother taught me the art of karate and I was going to show her how it felt for a bone to be broken in her body. When she walked up, I had to stand up so I got out of the vehicle and took my stance. She started coming towards me and said, "You think you know that stuff, umm!" I did a roundabout house kick, which did surprise her. She began talking trash and said, "You used that on me, you will go to jail." I said, "Well you wanted it and you will get up." Then it was all talk because she couldn't walk the walk. I said, "What's your name?" She said "Rhonda." I said, "You are that ding bat that feeds that so-called man, Mr. Devil, all your children's food." She said, "He is my man." I said, "He talks about you like a dog and treats you worse, cussing you out and telling everyone you are a fool, he's using you. He walks into your house and takes what he wants, your kids are in need and he doesn't care about you. He lives with his wife and he doesn't want you." She said, "No he's not." I said, "Yes he is, do you know who he lives with?" She said, "No, but he told me his mom." I said, "That can't be, he lives with his wife and you're stupid, meanwhile, we have to do this job and you're making me late, or you can go back into that office and I'll do the job myself." She jumped into my vehicle and we took off, meanwhile she started talking shit and running her mouth, but I would quickly put her in check. Then each day it got a little better to work with her, and we started being friends; or so I thought. We used to help each other out. I've seen times when she didn't have anything to eat, and as a friend, I helped her and her children, but now she had this old no good man, I didn't like him and he didn't like me. I tried to help her and all he did was use her, but I had to back away from them. Whenever they had a fight or he mistreated her, she would call and tell me what was going on. I had to stay away from them because he was married, even if I felt it was wrong; I was going to stay out of that. She would not have to worry about me being her friend, and when she needed someone to talk too, it wouldn't be me. He knew that she would soon be getting some money, and he would spend it all. I was her true friend and happy that she was getting it and I didn't want any of it. When it happens, she better not come crying to me. She had been acting all funny like she was all that, I should have known when I met her; she was like that. When life brought her down, she would meet me on the way down again. That's why I don't trust people, what happened to true friends? Whenever I start thinking of people who used to be my friend as an associate, they don't see or hear from me anymore. Well I got to keep on keeping on; I have things to do and people to see. You know, I never do anything for myself and now it's time for me, while I save my pennies and go away from this town for a little while. Not to see people, but places. I long to have the warm sun beaming down on my face and embrace the remnants of the fresh air on an island. I often dream about this, but I will try to make it come true this time. I watched everyone get what they wanted and now it's my turn. I ran into Tim the other day and he brought back many good memories. Oh, how I felt being with him, he made me feel loved at one time…mmm. We had some fun, it was just lust, but we loved every minute of it. We met on a blind date, he wasn't there for me. My friend was trying to hook me up on a blind date, and that was something I never wanted to do. She brought two guys over to my house, and I said, "Bring them in." When she introduced me to her date we both looked at one another and locked eyes, we wanted to switch. He was bold and said, "Let's switch." We did and Tim was so romantic that night, we had so much fun. I used to show up at his house in just a long trench coat and my high heels, a bottle of wine and two glasses. Every time I would go to the security desk, the man would keep me there trying to hook up with me. I told him, "Buzz me in man, I got a date." He would call up and say to Tim, "This lady down here, she said you know her." Tim would say, "Stop playing and let my lady in." After months went by, he asked me to move in with him. I felt I needed more time to get to know him. Rhonda was the one that brought him over; but now she knows he doesn't want her anymore. Like I said, it was lust and I felt I was having a good time. I loved playing games, like slaves; but never would I let him tie me up, and he loved the games we played. Sometimes the moon would shine into the window, it was so romantic. Moonlight, wine and so much fun in that place, if walls could talk and he would howl. That penthouse was the best, it had the finest. I thought he had a lot of money because of where he lived and how he lived; he drove a big fine car too. He should have been the man of my dreams, but I didn't love him and he didn't like children. My children were older, but I still had two at home with me. He said to me, "Let your children live with your mom," and that's what made me back away from him. I found a house a long way from where I was living. I moved away, changed my phone number and that was that; until I ran into him again! But not before he ran into Rhonda first. He told her I did him wrong by moving away, but the love of my children was more important than a life with him. Some women would have jumped at it, but I always wanted my children and I wasn't going to give them up for no man, even if I could travel the world. Their love meant more to me, so bye, bye Tim. As he looked in my eyes, he told me he had looked for me and he loved the way I sang to him. It always put a smile on his face, but we were just two souls passing in the night, time to move on. As I look at my life, I don't think there was a true love for me, because I lived a promiscuous life. The men I knew all just wanted to have sex with me; just because that's the way I met and dealt with them. I got five to six calls a week, and the conversation always came back to sex. None of them wanted to settle down with me, and it made me so mad, but I took the responsibility for what I did. I was on that path of destruction and there were people who helped me by messing up my life, but at that time, I didn't care. As I think about many things, it wasn't all bad; I can smile about some of my life. The phone rang and it was Hanna, she wanted to talk and I went by. She was crying and began saying men are no good and she did something that she didn't feel good about. You know, even though I watched what folks did, sometimes they would come to me with their story. She felt that her man was cheating, and she started to follow him. She finally saw him with some girl in the park. They looked like new lovers, laughing, and talking like the perfect couple and they wanted the world to see it. Then one night she followed them to a hotel, and sat outside until they came out. She got home before him and just played it off. She asked him how was work; he said it was boring and hard and she said, "Poor baby." Well she had to find a way to get him back for lying and cheating on her. He used to hang with his best friend Mike; they had been close since they were children. She had to make something happen. He used to come by and see her husband, and he would look at her as if he wanted her, "If I could only get my hands on that…umm." She started going around where he was and they began to talk, with tears in her eyes, she told Mike how she thought her husband was cheating. Mike told her he was cheating. "Just last night he said he was with you, and you know we were talking about that time." He told her she was not the first one he messed with someone else and then she knew she had him. She was going to have sex with her husbands' best friend. They started dating and went a lot of places; he made sure she was having a good time. He was happy giving her all the attention her husband wouldn't. Then one night he told her, "You know ever since he brought you around, I've had my eye on you Hanna, I just love the way you carry yourself, and I'm not going to lie, I want you." She knew that this would happen. He told her they would meet and go to a hotel, and she got ready and went to meet him. He was there before her, and while on the phone he told her what room he was in. The door was cracked and she could hear soft music playing, and it smelled so good as she walked inside. The lights were off; candle lights were burning; baby did it up right. It was more than she thought it would be he knew how to treat a woman. She had a very good time, and then went home. She felt the way he held her oh so tight and kissed her so gently. Then she felt sorry that she did it, sorry for pulling him in, but not too sorry; because she confessed to her husband when he got home that she knew about his cheating and she just did his best friend. At first, he yelled and was mad, but then he looked at her and walked out of the door. She said she was crying, because he was the one that got her to that point, why did she feel she had to get him back? Its bitter sweet, was this the end of a marriage? She called Mike and he told her to come to him, and this was the start of a beautiful love affair. Not only was things going wrong in my life, most of my friends too. I watched and they were not living a good life all the time. Like they say, into everyone's life, bad things will happen. Meanwhile, somehow those crazy people who were always bothering had my phone number, and every weekend I got a call, there was heavy breathing and stupid talk asking me for someone else or making noise. Whoever it was, they didn't scare me, and they let me know that people are crazy. They thought if they continued to cause mayhem in my life, they got me, but they didn't have me, I will make it through this like I have all the other times. Who in their right mind thinks a call will scare someone, they judged themselves and they thought it was me. I can choose not to answer the call and waste their time, so late at night; I turned my phone off. Then they started a daytime thing, calling, and talking crazy. They acted like they were crying and were sick, they had some nerve, what if they were sick for real, would I believe it? People playing on the phone are crazy, if that person does have an emergency that might not catch it in time, because they think dumb things are funny. They're thinking with their behind and not their head. Today I felt my worse and Joel showed up, and he was just what the doctor ordered. He held me close and comforted me as I told him everything I was going through. This day, my whole life was a mess, I was sick of carrying this load by myself, paying my own bills, being lonely all the time, having to take care of running my household. Sometimes a woman needs a man for his strength. She needs him to hold her when the going gets rough; you know what I'm talking about? Because a man needs a woman too, when your back hurts, you need someone to rub it. Joel is that kind of guy, but he is temporary, he wants to be everyone's everything, and that's spreading it to thin. He came in and I told him, "Joel, it's not going to be a hit and run this time," but he still tried. When we were teens, he was heavy petting me, but I said no and I meant it. Just because I was hurting, don't think the sex will help me, why do men think that is the key to life? I didn't want that, I needed to be hugged, not sexed. Comfort to a woman and comfort to a man are two different things so I made him leave. Today I found out that there's a place now that molested people can go, but the people who had to live through it without those helpful resources, were broken for life, because we have already made all the mistakes there are to make. If there would have been counseling back then, we would have handled things in a different way, because I was on a path of destruction, and sometimes I'm paying for now. It just made me feel like I was not as good as other people when I was young, and to this day, I don't trust anyone. Many of my friends couldn't take it anymore and have lost their mind, because they always thought they were no good or no one loved them. It made it hard to commit to any relationship. There were always fragments of themselves, doing all kinds of things to hurt themselves. People from my past kept coming up, but I didn't want to see them or talk to them, yet they kept popping up. No one seemed to care about people's feelings anymore. They walk all over everyone, like we are all just pieces of meat, hearts are broken, lives are messed up and most people won't even say they are sorry. Love is a hard thing to get over; some folks never recover from the pain of a break up, they just become numb, like I feel. Often, I find myself looking off into space, or just going through the motions every day, acting like I feel something but I can't feel anything anymore. Every time I think back on love, it hurts so bad and I don't want to hurt anymore. Then there are the times I'm so lonely I could scream, but who would hear me or even care? Loneliness puts you in a bad place; you start thinking of all types of things to do. I always thought about Joel, and if I called he would come over. But like I said, it's only for a little while, after the act is over, he gets on my nerves and I put him out.

CHAPTER TWELVE – WE ARE GETTING BEAT UP

There are so many ladies getting beat up! My dear friend Mary got gun butt until they found her dead. Jeana got her baby kicked out of her on the streets, while my husband held me back. I wanted to stop him and help; I saw the fetus coming out of her. Lee Lee's man stabbed her and she almost died, so many of us took too much. My husband used to kick me into next week, until I did something about it. One of my daughters used to get beat up all the time, until her children told me. I went over there and hit the guy she was seeing on the head and knocked him out, he never hit her again. We have the right to defend ourselves when someone is trying to hurt us. Many of my friends would call me after they have been beat up. Millie had a whole boot imprint on her face, I cried with her when I saw that. I've seen black eyes, swollen lips, bleeding heads and cuts on many parts of the body. If that is love, I don't want it. One lady had her arms and one leg broken, and he put her in the trunk of his car, he said he was giving her time to cool off. Is this how the man who says he loves you treats you, do you think he does, your choice should be to walk away from the violence. Whenever I'm feeling down and out, that Joel rears his head again, always smiling up around me. Every time he came around, it was only for one thing, trying to fight it was very hard, since I was in need and he knew it. I tried to fight the feeling, but sometimes, it's just so Ooooh! That's why I was always yelling and screaming at him, trying to fight that old feeling, and trying not to give in to it. It has been almost ten years and we still deal with each other. He has helped me through many things, but he won't commit. My life in a nut shell is it normal or is it messed up? There were some men I knew who were beaten up, I've seen my share of abuse and none of it was good. A friend of mine would repeatedly beat up her man, he was a drunken mess and she beat on him. They would go out to nice restaurants and turn the place out, until people called the police on them. He always looked like he lost the fights, his face all bruised, bleeding, black eyes and he couldn't go to work because she beat him so bad, and do you think he left? Sometimes I thought he loved it, sometimes when things in our childhood go wrong, we take anything, then we get old and there is no place to go or we would feel all alone. I used to wonder why some older people said, they didn't have time for the bull or they were afraid to get into another relationship, now I know why. It's like I can't sleep at night. Now I'm walking the floor all night and I didn't know why. The doctor didn't know why, but they wanted to give me meds, they felt like that was the cure for everything; keeping me drugged up. My husband called, and it had been a little while since I've heard from him. All he wants to do is use me, I'm sick of him; he only calls when he needs something. That's all I am to him, someone to bail him out when he's in trouble. The kids say, "Mom let him sleep in the bed he made." But I don't want to do wrong for wrong, because what did I teach my children all these years, be kind to people even if they don't treat you right. Granny told me that, and I try to be good, because she said, "You'll reap what you sow." He called me and said, "Can you come help me, my car has broken down." I wanted to say, "No I can't help you," but I said "ok." I took Jolina with me; I had to go a long way outside of the city to get to where he was located. He flagged me down, I pulled up and he already had his hood open. This lady walked out after the car started, I looked at her and he said, "I have to leave the car, it won't move, it's not just the battery it's the transmission." I said to myself, "Who is this lady, maybe she works at this motel where his car had stopped on him." Then he said, "I'm going to leave it for the tow truck, can you take me home, oh and my friend too?" My eyes got bigger than they were, and I said, "This is the reason I can't be with you, you're a cheater and you'll never change." She said, "Can you please take me back to the city, my husband would kill me if I had to call him and he finds out where I am and who I'm with." My mouth just dropped, I didn't like this, but I could not leave her out there by herself. No buses ran that late and I said, "Get in." As I got close to her house she said, "Let me out here, thank you." I just looked at my husband and said, "She's married too?" He didn't talk much; I never knew where he was staying. Then he said, "I can't give you any money, because I don't have any money on me." I said, "You better bring some to me when you get the chance, and he said, "Let me out here." I still didn't know where he lived and I didn't care, this is what I had been dealing with in the past, his cheating and hitting me. When he got out of the car, I screamed in my car and Jolina just laughed at me as I sobbed. That made me have flash backs of how I made clothes for the hoe he was going with when we broke up. Always been cheating, she used to bring her kids over and I would keep them and she would pay me. Her kids were very clean and well mannered; she must have told them not to tell me that my husband was at their house all the time. She would have me make her clothes, little short skirts. She paid me for them, but he was paying for all of that, that money was supposed to be coming into our household. He was doing me like a dirty rug, wiping his feet on me and laughing behind my back. Then that hoe got on those drugs very bad, they began to go down and they reaped it. He would call me and tell me things about her. I saw her all high in the streets. She fell down a few times, to the fact that she couldn't stand, the drugs took a toll on her. I've been catching hell for years, because I had a husband that didn't care or love me like a man is supposed to love his wife. If I needed something fixed, I had to fix it, if I needed food in the house, I had to get it, when my bills were unpaid, the bill collectors called me. I was doing everything by myself, I can't possibly be married, for real; where is my help? He brought a washer and dryer; she sold it for drugs while he was at work. He did so much more for her, but it's me that became his floor mat, or I'm just the back end of a mule when it comes to him. I said I am sick of him, when he gets in a bind, I help him. If he was the man I needed, my life would have been different. He would have been there for me, and our children wouldn't have suffered, but he chose to do what he wanted. He was so selfish and we got the short end of the stick. He gave me money for gas after I ran him all over town, and told me he wanted it back; after it was in my tank. If he thought I was going to run him all around, he was going to get a rude awakening. Some of the things I did because I had no love from him, he owes me more than I can count. He was always trying to use me, and I let him get away with it most of the time. Joel called and we were going to meet up, he somehow knew when I needed someone, because he would call or show up just when I needed someone to vent too. This time we were going out of town together. I packed my bags and we were going on a train trip down south. He showed up to get me, and he was looking good; this time he was dressed up. We went to the train station and got on the train. This was something I always wanted to do and he knew it. I know he was saying to himself, "I'm getting something for this." As we were riding on the train, there were lots of things we saw as we were sight-seeing, and it was just like I imagined, we had a good dinner, night time was coming and I wanted to sleep for a while. We went into our train car and he didn't try to touch me at all, just a kiss good night. Joel thought he was smart, but he was just helping me because I wanted this trip to be nice, no yelling or crying. I was going to make him pay for this, he'd better work hard to get it or he won't. I knew him, if I pissed him off bad enough, he wouldn't want to do anything, but this time, he was a gentleman. It was early morning when I woke up, we were pulling into our stop and we went to our hotel; and it was nice. I said, "Joel, where did you get the money for this?" He said, "Just enjoy it and don't ask questions." We were in Miami, oh this is nice, and that's what I said about the room we were in. Joel kissed me and said, "Put that red dress I got you on, the sandals and that hat, it's in my bag, I know what you like." I said, "You know just what I like, thank you for this trip." I kissed him on his face, showered, got dressed and we were out. It was early and we walked on the beach, not too many folks were out that time of day. I had fun talking to him and he made me laugh, this was feeling so good, I'm going to not want to go back home. He had a bag with him, and in it he pulled out a blanket that folded up, two glasses of wine. He laid the blanket down, opened the wine, we both took sips and I said, "Good wine." I looked at him and he kissed me softly and I kissed him back. I said, "I will always love you Joel, not just because we have a child together, but I fell in love with you when we were young, I watched you from across the street, all the time not knowing that we would hook up some day." He said, "Once again, I love you in my own way." I never knew what that meant, in my mind; you do or you don't. He began to kiss me on my legs, and he kissed me all up under my dress; he always knew how to make me feel good. As things began to happen, I heard a voice say, "Umm, get a room please, other folks use this beach." He pulled his head from under my dress, and we both looked up and it was an older lady speaking to us, all we could do was laugh. I said, "Joel, you dog, you had me forgetting we were outside."

We got up and walked down the beach, and he said, "Let's go back to the room" and I said, "Ok." We had a hot tub and we finished the wine while we were in the hot tub. Joel said, "Let's take a nap before lunch time." We laid down to go to sleep, he held me in his arms as we fell asleep. I thought, what's wrong with him, Joel is not like this, he's used to getting it and not wanting to wait; what! I hope he is not sick or dying, that would hurt my heart. When we woke up it was a little past lunch, but we ordered something anyway and the food was good. After that he just kept kissing me and looking in my eyes. I wanted to ask him what was wrong, but I wasn't going to mess this up. He said, "Get dressed; we got a lot to see here." He had planned the whole trip and we were having so much fun, still he didn't say he wanted sex. Well was he going to ask me to marry him or what, why was he so different now? Joel has shown me a good time, we had been there for three days, and not once did he try to have sex with me. Oh my! Ok, somethings up, he was acting very much out of character. This was not Joel, did he bump his head, is he all right, and I couldn't bring myself to ask him, I was afraid of his answer. We went out on the town, club hopped until morning and then we went back to our room. Then he said, "Let's talk and I said "Ok," we ordered food and talked. He said, "I love you very much, and not just because we have a child, I've been in love with you for a long time; you don't think I do, but I don't know how I could live with you and only you. I've been used to having so many women and I don't know how to stop. We have had a good time together, but how; tell me now can I remain true? I've been hurting you and everyone I tried to get serious with for years, this is a problem. That's why I didn't want this trip to be about sex. Tell me what to do, it's time for me to settle down and stop tricking and having many women. I know you were asking yourself what's wrong with me, well there; you know." My mouth just dropped, what am I going to do about this?

CHAPTER THIRTEEN – THIS IS ANOTHER FINE MESS YOU GOT ME INTO

It was time to get back to work and I got my things ready for the next day. Lee Lee came by, my house, she was mad with her kids and she had to leave for a while. She said she hadn't heard from me in about a week, and I didn't want to talk about it. I said, "I need a stiff drink" and she said, "What's wrong with you?" She knew I didn't drink, and it had been over ten years since I took a drink. I don't drink anymore, but not long ago I did, but she didn't know about it. She said, "You must need to talk more than I do." We went to get some food, sat there, and talked; it was about her life, not mine. I took a deep breath and said, "I'm sleepy, got to go to work, got to go home," and I did and that was that. I had some choice words going around in my head. The next day I didn't want to talk to anyone. I was sitting alone thinking about all the things I've been through. It won't do any good to ask why, I'm not going to get an answer; somehow, I must learn from them. Let me see, I don't trust, I don't care anymore, I don't like some people, but there are some good things still in my life, and they make me happy. I don't want to die, don't get it twisted. It was a gray rainy day and I was going to see my sister. When I got to their house, they were in an up roar, fighting, cussing, and swinging at each other. They didn't even see me walk in, then I said, "Well, hello!" She looked at me and said, "Come on in." Her husband and child walked out of the room, they didn't even speak. I said, "Uh uh, what's going on?" She said, "I can't stand them sometimes, they think I'm supposed to do everything in this house, I work too hard and they don't think I'm worth it; I'm just broken, what's been up?" I just looked at her and said, "You don't want to know." We had lunch and talked about being young, and then we began to cry. We have been wronged so much in this life, and that made us pick these lives. I thought maybe her and I needed that good long cry. We talked a little longer and I said, "Got to go," and I went home; and guess who was sitting on my steps, Joel. I looked at him and said, "No, this is not the time, go home and get away from me." He looked at me and said, "I'll come back when you want to talk," and I slammed the door in his face. I was pissed and no tear would fall from my eyes, what was I going to do about this mess with him? Weeks went by and I hadn't heard from or called him, and I felt he was truly gone. Why would someone tell you that they can't be true and that you are going to stay with them, can you trust someone like that? Should you give them a chance to do it, or just leave them alone? Just thinking about this made me wonder, did those people who are tearing my stuff up forget about me. No one had done anything to my car or my house lately. Did they have a revelation, or just saw that they were getting no place with that, because I've found a way through those things and I've had total peace. I still have feelings when things are going to happen, but they are getting few and far between. Maybe this book is what helped me see those things in a different light. You know what I think, I'm going to call up Joel and give him a second chance. Then I won't be alone anymore, he said he loved me and maybe we can work it out. Oh, I heard a knock at the door; I looked out the window and saw who it was; It was my old good friend Max. Now I want you to scratch that line I just said about Joel. I opened the door and said, "Come on in, the last time I saw you, I ended up with that pulled muscle, we laughed and were wrestling around and I pulled it." That killed the whole mood; I had to go to the hospital. They put me through all kinds of tests, I was in tears and it felt like a heart attack, oh the pain. They kept asking me what happened, and no one would believe I was just playing around and pulled my muscle like that. I called Rosa and she laughed so hard, she wouldn't believe me and wanted to know just how it happened. A few other friends wanted to think I was put in weird position, they kept saying that must have been some bad sex, who put it on you? They wouldn't believe the truth, see I had a reputation. Anyhow he's here, and come on in Max. Whenever I needed to talk, he was there. Back in the day, we went out together and got drunk, shopped, and just hung out and did all girly things. Sometimes I used to think he was the one, but he was just a very good friend. We never had anything to do with each other, people used to think we were, but no; just friends. I said, "Well tell me what's been going on." He had left town with some girl, they were going to get married and he said that was the worst thing that happened to him. He took her to his hometown to meet his family and they stayed there. He got a job and they began to live together. She got a job too, and became so Boo Chee-Ghetto. When they were here, she was a hot mess, she would totally embarrass him. She dressed like a hoe, she talked like a hoe, she acted like a hoe, and if it smells like and looks like it; it's got to be a hoe. That poor man, his family would call him and tell him what she was doing, they were watching her every move. What made him leave was because she liked to go out and drink a lot; well she couldn't keep her clothes on and loved to dance naked. One night he got a call from his cousin to come down to the bar where she was at. It was about closing time and they locked the door and let everyone else out. He didn't see her, but his cousin said she was still there, so they started the music and she came out of the back dancing. It was dark lightsome and she didn't see him and she started out dancing on the pole. The males left inside the club started yelling and howling. His cousin held him back and said, "Wait and watch what she is doing." She started to take off her clothes; the men were feeling all on her, she was butt naked. He yelled, "No you dirty, put them clothes back on." She saw it was him and his cousin, he grabbed for her and she grabbed her clothes and ran into the back. He said, "So this is your job, we are through, you acted like I had the problem when it was you." Tears filled his eyes as he told me this story and I pulled him into my arms and held him close. She had brought a grown man to tears, I felt so bad for him. I said, "Ok, let's change the subject; I'm sorry you had to live with that, let me get you some food and let's hang out here." We talked and he calmed down. I went into the guest room to fix it up for him and he went back to watch a movie. I kissed him softly as I held him close; he needed that; and a lot of hugs. Sometimes we all need someone to hold and comfort us. As I thought back and watched people, we all needed the same thing, love to sustain us, because you don't do well in life if there is no love. Max had been beaten and brought down so low, and I felt sorry for him. I loved him and he had been my friend for years. After a while I said, "I got to go to work in the morning Max, you can stay long as you want, you can turn off everything; see you in the morning." Then I left him in the living room, took a hot bath and went to bed. I turned off my lamp and my door opened and Max stood there. I said, "Come to bed," and I guess you know what happened then, we both felt we were soul mates. The next day I got a call from my friend name Willow, one of our friends had killed her husband. I knew she used to come to work with all kind of bruises, black eyes and cuts all over her. She was a good mom and loved having her children and being married, but he abused her. He kicked her in the head, slapped her and punched her, she couldn't help but to snap, but it was oh so wrong how it happened. She had just come home from a stress filled day at work, he began beating her up. She ran into the kitchen, got a sharp knife, and went to work on him, stabbing him some one hundred times all over the body and face. Her children saw her kill their dad and they cried. Some of the police couldn't stand the sight they saw, and began throwing up at the sight of blood all over. She stabbed him until he didn't move anymore; you could hardly tell what he looked like. She even stabbed him in the eye; his abuse would cause her to get the rest of her life behind bars and the children mentally unstable for life. Abuse will kill you and those around you. I saw those cases of abuse all the time, and it made me sick because I started having flashback of what happened to me. I had met a man and we began to talk, but I wouldn't let him get to close to me. He was always telling me he wanted me, and I took it with a grain of salt. He took me to lunch, dinner and we even went to some movies, but every time I began to talk, he would tell me to shut up. I would stop talking before I said too much. I said to myself, "All that he is doing for me is not worth it, verbally he was abusing me." One day he told me how he would beat other women if they didn't shut up, and I obeyed him. Then he said he was cussing them out and called them all kinds of names. One day he told me to shut and I almost snapped, but I stopped myself. I took him for a ride in the country, way out from the city and looked for a place to bury him, yes, I said bury. I was going to kill him, but I thought no, I turned around and went back to his house and dropped him off. I didn't answer his calls or the door when I saw him again. He caught me coming from work and tried to talk to me. I said, "If you value your life, you will not talk to me, do you value your life?" He gave me the strangest look and turned and walked away. Verbally, he was going to make me kill him, after years of abuse I couldn't take it anymore. With each one of those people, I knew; I knew something wasn't right. Some people I would tell and some I wouldn't tell my business too. They wouldn't believe that some people had the powers to tell them what might happen in their life or wouldn't happen. Sometimes I looked in their faces and saw something wasn't right, abused people have this look on their face, even if they try to hide it. My friend Anna was a nice lady; she ate, walked, and talked only when her man told her too. She went to work and home and no other place unless he wanted her to go. If she said he was going out with friends, they had to be the ones he liked. If he told her not to talk to people, she would not, she acted like he could see long distance and didn't talk to some people because he would beat her up. Sometimes the neighbors would have to call the police; he would beat her all the way out into the street and drag her back into the house for more. She had broken ribs and a broken arm. She let this happen because she had no mom to tell her what she should or should not take from a man. The court took her from her mom and gave her to her dad, because mom didn't have the money. She was a broken woman, when she was young, that stepmom beat her when her father wasn't home. One day while he was at work, she backed a truck up to the house and put everything on the truck and left his clothes on the floor. He didn't even have a bed to sleep on. He asked the people next door if they saw her take everything and they said no. Some laughed and said, "Good, I know where she went, but I would never tell him, he would just abuse her again." Don't get me wrong, I didn't tell any of them to do this, they just did it, and we all have shared our stories. We were all broken women, but we started out as broken girls. People we need to change the way we treat each other, your significant other is not your slave, you're supposed to love each other, not hit, or beat on each other. The children coming from those homes are mentally sick; they need to go to counseling. They have all kinds of things wrong with them, because of the way they have been treated. If someone ever treated you bad, I say get some help before you kill them or they kill you, or you're beaten until you lose your mind. Some men think their dog is better than their wife, and will treat them better. The one I married, I don't even know where he lives or what he does. Often our children ask where he is and I don't know. I've been sick and in the hospital and he never showed up. Even if they are grown, the children should have had their dad in their lives, they could never depend on him. There have been times when I didn't have food in the house and we didn't know how to get in touch with him. He would come around when that girl was off on her binge, but we had not seen him for three years and we are in the same city. Jolina's dad was there, Joel was too nosey to get lost and I had to tell him to leave a lot. The few times I tried to go back to my husband, it was because the kids asked me too, but each time he would abuse me and I'm not having that anymore. But I tell you, he got what was coming to him, that woman was broken too. She was on crack so bad, I would see her lying on the ground high, and men did all kinds of things to her. She used to steal his money. One day he tried to hit her like he did me and her children jumped on him and beat him up. When he went to visit his mom, she would sell everything she could, and then he started coming over or calling and telling me about it. He made his bed and he had to sleep in it, but it didn't hit hard, he just moved on to something else bad. The kids saw him with her driving by and he kept going. Now all the holidays and birthdays he missed, I tried to comfort my children and hope that they make their lives better than what they came from, may God have mercy on them. My oldest son told me his wife was broken too and that soon ended. She wanted to fight him all the time, he told her he had seen too much of that at home and couldn't stand it and he left her. I think back on when I was so badly treated, and I smile now because Max is here, we will go on in a loving, peaceful life, but so many will die or go crazy or even kill someone. I hope this book helps you get through everything you may be going through; it should help you to realize that you're not alone; there are so many others out there. I'm letting you know that you can have a better life, things can work out for you; just don't let anyone hurt you and disrespect you ever again. If you need of help, get some.

Why do so many men rape and molest girls when there are so many grown women out there ready to give them what they want? It hurts me so much every time I hear another woman or girl tell me what they are going through. When I meet someone, I could tell something has happened to them. They are all sad, but some ladies are broken and just accept it, it makes you kind of become numb. When I was young, people used to say, get over it, it didn't kill you; people are said you'll be all right. The very act of someone forcing himself on you messes up your mind. That's something I get mad about, when you have a family member do something you never thought they would do. One day my nephew came to talk to about a problem he was having. The system was thinking about taking his daughter so he wanted to know if she could stay with me for a while until he straightened things out. So, I did let her stay. Now listen to this story because it gets worst. He was smooth and calm with it, at birth his child's mom didn't want her, their relationship was bad and they always fought. Sometimes it looked like everything was ok, but it wasn't. I was called for intervention, so I talked to a worker and she started to tell me some things was going on. Well it turned out; they told me some funny things were going on in his household. I listened and my blood began to boil. Her mother had given him total control and she signed all her rights over to him, she wanted nothing to do with the child or him. While in his care, he did this and he knew she was already messed up in the head because of her mom. Why she was just a little rag to him, my heart went out to this little girl. He tried to blame it on the death of his father, like it just made him so insane. I have seen so many things that are wrong from birth, his mom treated him like he was nothing and that treatment got passed down to the next generation. Children trust their parents, but some of them need to be feared. He didn't like the way I ran my house, but he's going to have to get used to it, I had to put my foot down. He thought because I'm soft hearted, he could run all over me, but when it comes to abuse; I'm like a bull that will gore him to death and won't blink an eye. This poor girl can't do many things for herself, and I need to pick up the pieces of her life so she can be a better person. There was no line drawn, and I needed to help fix that without hurting her more; this is a thin line. I want her to trust me, but not the kind of trust he's shown, because right now she has blind trust and that's not good. Since she was younger, she has been groomed to let anything happen and they don't like to follow rules. On one hand, some things are good they have taught her, and on the other hand there were bad things. She had been groomed to accept his advances, but reject someone else. He hits her and plays if off like it's a game. When I say "them" I'm talking about his mom, she messed him up. He doesn't feel the guilt that he should feel; I think she did that to him too. The touching and feeling on people is not right, and sex with a family member is a big no, no. When we were young, she used to always feel people up, people used to laugh it off. Now that she is old, she still doesn't see anything wrong with it. That kind of abuse is worse, because they groom the person and they don't see anything wrong with what some people view as wrong. I walked in my room one day, and there she was, naked to the world and he was looking at her, if I hadn't walked in, what would have happened? I yelled, "Get out of my room, what are you doing in the room while she's changing, get out I need to talk to you. You have no business in the room when a young lady is dressing; she's not your wife or your girlfriend." He tried to say he liked grown women, but he's been without a woman for a long time. Now I knew why he had groomed his child to do what a woman would do, nasty ass pervert. I blame his mom, because she made him like this, but he has been broken. He takes her to school and makes some of her life look good to others, but now we all know the story. She was a broken girl and didn't know it. Why hasn't he tried to move on with his life? I don't know any woman that is so obsessed with her child, that they overdue being a parent. They call it grooming, because the child is taught to do just what the parent likes. He took her to lunch and dates like she was his woman; she didn't know it was wrong because he's been doing this for years. So many ladies lived with this until they were old enough to break from him, when she finds out that he was wrong. That's when all the stuff will hit the fan, but he makes her feel like daddy loves her and would never do anything to hurt her. But she will need to talk to someone about her mental state in the future. His mom is helping him and other people are turning a blind eye to what's going on. Trying to talk to social workers is not going anywhere, they said they need to have a child come right out and tell them what's going on, but that's not going to happen when they are groomed. He had so much power over her, when she got older she would tell her story too, and it would be swept under the rug. I ran into all kind of road blocks when I tried to do something about what I saw. They told me when I caught him in the bathroom as she was taking a bath that he was allowed in there, even when she was twelve years old. They said even if her dad walked around the house in the nude, it's just something they do in their house and some families thought it was all right. He acted like a dog smelling her up all the time. I knew that something was going on, but there's nothing I could do about it, this was the worst kind of abuse and I had to walk away from it. It would have to work itself out, one day she will tell. There are so many cases like this, and many other things going on that never get reported and never get told. I felt so sick inside when I thought about it. For you who are reading this book now, I hope that you find peace in your life; you can move ahead and live. It's the "what if" that never had to happen to me, that will hunt you until death. In this last story, that girl was the third generation in her family that it happened too, and no one says anything. No one can do anything, so I held my head down and walked away. I can't say anything, but I have a feeling and think about the things she told me. Lately I've been consumed with these other lives, and maybe my friend Max has been neglected. While he was at work, I made dinner, got some candles, and brought a bear skin rug. I pushed back the bed, got the glasses and the wine, and put on some soft music. I waited for him to walk in the door. The lights were low, I heard the key and I had his bath all ready. I said, "Come on in, I got everything ready for you." I'm still a broken woman, but its times like this that help me stay sane. We had a lovely time that night, we were so thankful we found each other; we were each other's equilibrium. Max will always be my friend. I'm trying to keep a level head about things that is going on, there are so many road blocks and they keep me from doing the right thing and the wrong thing. All the things I wanted to do, I let people keep me from doing, I'm wondering where do I go from here; I must push forward. I've been lied too, pushed around, done wrong, mistreated and hurt so much in this life, and did these things help me or hurt me, would I have been better than I am or worse? Abuse is so ugly and it hurts, so many won't tell their story and act like it never happened. I hope this makes you all keep your head high and live past all the bad things. I didn't write some things because it hurts too badly. It would hurt someone who could not bear it, or others knowing it would mess up someone's good life they have now, or it will open some sad places in their hearts. I had a chance to help a little girl who as going through some things. She had been abused until the point of insanity. I had to let her go before I went crazy, because no matter what you say to her, the abuser is always right. As she gets older, she will realize every wrong thing and every right thing. I hope she remembers a better way to live. They gave her back to her abuser, but they said he has gets counseling, what kind of justice is that? He doesn't have to stop the abuse, he will just keep it silent, now she won't tell because she feels it would hurt him. She loves him and don't want him to go to jail. She made the statement to me she didn't want him to go to jail. She feels she can live a little different, this may or may not be true, but now she knows there is a difference after talking to me. As I share my life, there are some more things being told to me, boys have been broken too, but that's another story. I'm glad I started talking about this, it helped me to let go of so much pain and I will press on. The more I talk to everyone, the more I find things out. There are so many ladies that are in these situations, it hurts me every time I hear that so many girls are broken. What is it about a little girl that makes a grown man have sex with a child, when I know there are so many grown women out there who wants a man. What is this sickness wanting little girls, is it that they don't fight back? Some women don't fight back; some just let men do just what they want. Why mess up a little child's mind? I often look back at myself, when I'm in a mood; I see me happy and so intense, all this knowing things happening before it did, and becoming that man's piece of joy. This is what he said, but me, not knowing why. I would look up at his face, I saw him make ugly faces, I didn't know if he hurt or felt good, why? After I was told this was nasty and wrong, I felt something wrong with me or did I do anything to make this happen. I thought about all the others, did they feel it was their fault too, and some went crazy. I began to talk to my mom about the things that happened to me and she began to cry. I said, "Don't cry mom, I got this, it doesn't have me." She began talking about my dad, for years I pressed her about him and she would tell me different things, like he ran away to California and died. She told me of the night I was conceived. She went to his apartment to a party, when she got there, she was the first to come. Now she had been dating him and knew he was older, but he was acting like a gentleman, until that night. He said to her, "Let's dance, the others will come, so let's enjoy this party while we are waiting." They danced and no one came, soon she found out no one was coming. He wanted her and told her of a party, he began kissing and holding her and she wanted to go. He started to pull and tug at her clothes; he pushed her down and raped her. "Oh, my God she is telling me, after all these years, and all I've been through; that I am a child born from rape. No wonder she didn't want to talk about it. I do remember him coming to see me when I was young and going to his mom's house, but they all moved away and I never saw him again. His life was more important than that little girl he deflowered, the girl he raped. My mom raised me by herself and then she met her husband, the father of my other brothers and sisters; the rest of the story is in this book. I think about my life more, how I have a husband that don't love me, how I'm left to fend for myself. I get so mad, because I don't have anyone to lean on, after being an abused broken child; I need someone here for me. I feel like I pay every day, because I wasn't told some things or taught how I should live, or bits and pieces of happiness I saw; my mom have. Now that I'm in the twilight of my life, I'm feeling more lost than I've ever been. I'm always longing for that warm feeling of someone holding me tight and making me feel safe. Looking for love in all the wrong places and making so many mistakes. We, the children who have been abused, are always looking in the wrong places for love. There have been times when you think you have it, and it turns out oh so bad and my heart is once again sad. I don't want to live my life by myself, but it looks like I will. I don't want to run into someone that will treat me any kind of way. I don't ever want to be beat up and mistreated again. I have been told my husband can treat everyone like a queen, but me. He's been telling people he and his girlfriend are private people and they don't want everyone to know their business. (My thoughts), *Well I got news for you boo boo, you don't have any business! You have children that barely see you, some you never told your family about her or her about them, you are a poor excuse for a man. You are an insult to me, I helped you along and you mistreated me every time you got a chance. He made me feel like I didn't want a relationship anymore, but life is all good to you. I'm thinking that all men are all going to be like you. I was on my sick bed and he never came to see me, the one I gave myself to in marriage. So many ladies let what happened in the past rule their lives today, never getting past what happened to them. I choose to go the other way, it happened and I must live my life. I can't let the past kill me, because it will. I found out there is a time and a place for everything under the sun, we must find happiness in ourselves and move on. Yes, to be molested makes you feel nasty, unloved, torched and like you are nothing, but you are someone and you can be loved. You can live past all the hurt, just try it one day at a time and you'll see; you got it, it doesn't have me. Keep your head up. Sometimes in my life, I feel that I've always been mistreated from the time I was a young broken girl until now. I've told people to don't let your past interrupt your future, you live life and that's what I try to do. All the wrong that was done to me, I feel like I should be bitter, but I'm not; I just go on living.* Oh, my God! I received some more bad news. I got a phone call, Lee Lee was crying, her niece was 5 years old and had been molested by her own dad, how can people just be so nasty? He laid her down and pushed himself up inside of her and didn't care about the crying and screaming. He was taping it to show other people, don't know if he sold it or not. He made a movie of himself raping his own child, what is this world coming too? While looking through his things, the child's step mom found it and started to watch it. When she saw the video tape she went looking for him. She had noticed the little girl was acting strange lately; that's why before she told him she knew, she called the police. When the police got their she turned on the movie he made, they put him in handcuffs and took him away. He claimed that drugs made him do that. Now we have one more to add to the broken, then her cousins said he did them like that. So many ladies have been living with this and not having anyone to talk too about it, it's been swept under the rug too much, when will this end? It caused some of us to act out so bad, because you're feeling used, abused and unloved, you just get on that path of self-destruction. Ladies watch your little girls, because just like me and the other girls, that molester is right around the corner. You may trust him, but you had better check him out good. He may act like he's the best step dad or dad in world, but maybe the nasty man is in your little girl's life. Mothers talk to your girls, there may be some things they would tell you, but if they feel they can't talk to you, then what? Not only girls, but sometimes boys, but that's another story. This world is sick; they may fall prey to someone too. The future of the world rests on the children, and if they are all messed up in the mind, what will the world be like in the years to come. I find myself looking at people and wondering what their story is, we all have one. I often find myself in my own little fantasy world. As a child; I grew up happy, both mom and dad were there. I was happy, they loved me and gave me what I wanted, they showed me love and there was nothing wrong in my life. I go to school and college, meet someone that I marry and love and he loved me too with all his heart. We began to have a family; life is so wonderful and we live happy ever after. This is that lie a lot of us are told, some don't even get that story. What we see and live around paints a very different story. I laugh and I have my good moments, but what is this life about? I'm looking at how much my husband hates me. He came to me for many things, but only using me, he messed me and these kids up. I teach them to love everyone, but he makes it hard. He waited until the children were grown and said he wanted DNA testing. I've been through hell with him. Everything I did for him up until today and in the past day, he tore me down; why doesn't he just love me? If I had been that dirty hoe, maybe he would have. He has lost his damn mind; he wants to sue me, for what? I'm the one that helped him even when he flashes his hoes in front of my face and he would hurt me because she said so. I look at people who are in good marriages and wonder why didn't I get that? I can smile, but it hurts me when I say things like that. After one man in a marriage, I will never do it again, but for real, I've never done it and this was far from happy. He met me young and broke this broken woman more. I wanted a good life with all the fixings and that never came my way; just always beat downs, why? I'm not the only one that feels this way; there are so many asking why. I'm feeling like everything I wanted in my life was the wrong things, because of the internal things I would feel inside. I didn't think that I wanted true happiness, only a way to escape my past. I wanted something that never came to; I let the past help me tear some of it up. There are things I want to write, but it will be too painful, more than just what happened to me, but that I caused. Self-hatred is very hard thing to accept, there was a time when I felt it. Then I looked at everything and I can't hate me for the things others done to me. Then I found self-love, others saw this and wanted to tear me down, because they had self-hate of their own, only hurting others made them feel much more than me. People told me I must find peace, virtue, and love, after being through so much; I don't know that I've found all that. I do have peace in some parts of my life, and to write this down on paper helped me so much, and love to a degree. I've been told that finding God will help me find out what my purpose is here, because I don't think I've found it yet. Been looking at many things, but now I'm sick and there's not much I can do. I get mad because some of my healthy days are gone, thinking everything I've gone through helped me get this way. All the stress and pain I held inside of me helped it along. I felt I was handling it, but often I let it hurt me more. I will end this, but there will be more. I think about my step dad and how before he died he begged me to forgive him as he passed over, he yelled and I said "I will never forgive you for what you've done to me," I don't know if I have. Those were the last words he heard from me, it changed so many things in my life and in my heart. I believe people don't love each other, that true kind of love, romantic and sweet kind of love. Wish I could have been proven wrong, but here it is, this book is yours.

THE END

P.S. I keep feeling if someone would come along that love me they I was supposed to be loved, they would have made this broken life worth something, worth living, but it's just one of them dreams. I hate the fact that I always had to fend for myself. This made me bitter once again; will I live the rest of my life broken?

FOOD FOR THOUGHT:

I AM ACHING…My heart is so, so heavy…and I hate when I feel edgy… but you made me feel this way…where is my heart? It's lost because of the choices you made…and all the things that I've allowed…Oh God! I need to be saved…this burden is too heavy…and I am so sick and tired that I need to worry…all I need and want is to be loved…will you help me…will you love me? I am aching…so bad that my internal organs are in pain…why did he leave me? Why did he hurt me? From this day on…I won't ever, never say his name…because of him playing games…it's hard for me to stay sane…Lord I am aching! Please save me today…

This is my contribute to the life of my mother Elaine Denise Robinson. She died before her time. She was a very wonderful person, it's so sad that she never found the love that she was looking for in a man. I want her to know that she has all the love and great memories from us. She started writing this book in 2010 and she finished in November of 2011 and she died on February 5, 2012, only 29 days after her 60th birthday. May her soul rest in peace as I release her book to the world. She is not only my mother; she is now all of yours. I love you mom and I will never, ever forget you, I thank you for being so tough and hard on me. I hope now you can finally be proud of me. You're missed deeply by family and friends. THANK YOU FOR LEAVING YOUR STORY WITH US, WE SHALL CHERISH IT FROM GENERATION TO GENERATION!

Charles Lee Robinson Jr. & Elaine Denise Robinson

973·903-1540

973-226-1368 —
Delete

CPSIA information can be obtained
at www.ICGtesting.com
Printed in the USA
BVHW051417171218
535792BV00018BA/2438/P